BILLY MOON

BILLY MOON

DOUGLAS LAIN

TOR®

A TOM DOHERTY ASSOCIATES BOOK

NEW YORK

BILLY MOON

Copyright © 2013 by Douglas Lain

Edited by James Frenkel

A Tor Book
Published by Tom Doherty Associates, LLC
175 Fifth Avenue
New York, NY 10010

www.tor-forge.com

Tor® is a registered trademark of Tom Doherty Associates, LLC.

Library of Congress Cataloging-in-Publication Data

Lain, Douglas.
   Billy Moon / Douglas Lain.—First edition.
       p. cm.
   "A Tom Doherty Associates book."
   ISBN 978-0-7653-2172-5 (hardcover)
   ISBN 978-1-4299-4807-4 (e-book)
       1. Milne, Christopher, 1920–1996—Fiction.   2. Riots—France—
Paris—Fiction.   I. Title.
   PS3612.A466B55 2013
   813'.6—dc23

                                                          2013006424

First Edition: August 2013

Printed in the United States of America

0 9 8 7 6 5 4 3 2 1

Dedicated to the spirit of 1968. You reappeared briefly in 2011.
I'm keeping a candle in the window for you.

ACKNOWLEDGMENTS

There are two dead men who deserve acknowledgment here, although whether either would accept the association that this acknowledgment brings if they were still alive is an open question.

The first of the two is none other than the real Christopher Robin. Christopher Robin Milne managed to grow out of being a character in his father's books and transform himself into a character of his own. His memoirs *The Enchanted Places* and *The Path Through the Trees* tell the story of this character's struggle to formulate an identity and life beyond the world of Pooh. For those who are interested in what Christopher Robin and A. A. Milne's relationship might've "really" been like, these memoirs are the books to read. In any case, I recommend both of Christopher's books to you, my readers, and suggest that his story is yours and mine as well.

The second of the two dead men who deserve acknowledgment is the French radical theorist Guy Debord. Debord's championing of the practice of détournement, a technique whereby writings and artworks are derailed or twisted in new works that misquote the originals, made my twisting of Christopher Robin Milne possible.

There are others who must accept acknowledgment. Lisa Goldstein, whose novel *The Dream Years* twisted or derailed both the surrealists of the early twentieth century and the striking workers of May 1968, deserves recognition.

And there are more still. Henri Lefebvre, Françoise Sagan, Ralph Rumney, Robert Silverberg, Jean Luc-Godard, France

Gall, Brian Jones, and Daniel Cohn-Bendit all deserve a mention. Also traces of ideas from Karl Marx, Louis Althusser, Raoul Vaneigem, and Slavoj Žižek can be found here.

Fellow travelers M. K. Hobson, Eileen Gunn, Cameron Pierce, Alyx Dellamonica, Kris O'Higgins, Jim Frenkel, and Joan Vinge (who helped me learn to write many years ago) and many others deserve some blame here as well.

Finally, I want to acknowledge my wife, Miriam, who has patiently encouraged me to press on with this sort of thing.

PART ONE

1959–1965

In which Christopher Robin fails to escape his stuffed animals, Gerrard goes to the police museum, and Daniel is diagnosed with autism

1

Christopher was thirty-eight years old and still hadn't managed to escape his stuffed animals. Worse, the neighborhood stray, a grey British Shorthair, was scratching at the entrance of his bookshop. Chris looked up to see the cat making no headway on the glass but leaving muddy prints under the sign that was now flipped so that the CLOSED side was facing out for passersby to read. The cat's scratching made a repetitive and grating noise that reminded Chris of a broken wristwatch.

It was October 2, 1959, and Christopher was up early. It was his usual practice to enjoy these solitary early hours in the bookshop. He quite liked waiting for the teakettle to sound, looking out at the mist over the River Dart, and listening to the silence that seemed to radiate from the spinner racks full of paperbacks. He had the novel *On the Beach* by Nevil Shute open by the cash register and he was skimming it. The story had something to do with a nuclear war and a radioactive cloud, but the details weren't getting through to him. He just had twenty minutes or so before Abby would be awake, and he decided not to waste them on another literary apocalypse.

Chris had been getting up earlier and earlier, spending more and more time on the inventory sheets, keeping track of the invoices, and taking care of that local stray cat. Hodge—Christopher had named him Hodge—was an abandoned tabby actually, and not a British Shorthair at all. Hodge had been content to live over the bookstore and eat what Chris fed him, usually fat from a roast or bits of fish, outside on the boardwalk. At least, that had been the arrangement for nearly six months. Lately Hodge had been a little more demanding. He had, on occasion, even made his way inside the shop.

When the kettle sounded Chris poured the hot water into a bone china pot ornamented with blue flowers, waited for his breakfast tea to steep, then poured a cup and added cream and sugar. Only after all of this did he give in to the sound at the door, but by this time, Hodge had changed his mind. Chris opened the door and the cat wandered away, across the boardwalk and into the weeds. Hodge hadn't really wanted in at all, but maybe had just wanted Christopher's company out in the grey mist of the morning. It was impossible to say for sure.

He stepped back into the shop, slowly wandered down the main aisle, taking a moment here and there to note what books were still in place, which books had been on the shelf the longest, and when he reached the counter he wrote down the titles. He checked the ledger for the previous day and saw that the list of old books hadn't changed. J. P. Donleavy's *The Ginger Man* and Colin Wilson's *The Outsider* had been big sellers for several years, but perhaps Devon had run out of angst because he had three copies of each gathering dust.

Then Hodge was at the side window. The cat was sitting on a

waste bin under the store's green-and-white awning and was scratching away again, leaving more muddy paw prints.

Chris stepped outside again, onto the boardwalk, and walked around the corner of the shop to the waste bin. He reached down, hooked his hand around the cat's midriff, and carried him like that, with his legs and paws dangling, into the shop.

"I'll make up your mind for you," Chris said.

There was no point in trying to discipline a cat. You could try scolding, even give the animal a good wallop, but all that would accomplish would be a reaction, maybe get you scratched. The cat might scurry off between the bookshelves, look at you indignantly, perhaps even feign indifference, but the cat would never behave differently. Cats merely did what they did.

There was a stack of boxes behind the counter, a new shipment of children's books, but Chris hesitated to open them. For a moment, before opening the first one, Christopher remembered how the shop, his Harbour Bookshop, had looked before the first shipment of books arrived. When the shelves were bare they'd reflected the light coming in and the shop had seemed positively sunny. There was nothing in the bookstore but light, shadow, and the smell of sea salt.

Christopher opened the box of books and then felt a familiar anger welling up in him.

"Abby, you bloody well know that we don't sell *Winnie-the-Pooh*," he shouted into the stacks. His wife was upstairs, either still in bed or in the lavatory. She was spending a great deal of time on the toilet, even more than he'd originally expected when she'd told him she was pregnant. Wherever she was she surely couldn't hear him shout, but he was tempted to shout again, only louder. He let out a long sigh instead.

Christopher made his way up the stairs and called out again.

"Shall we ask the Slesingers and Disney to become partners in our bookstore? Shall we sell dolls and toys and records, all the Pooh paraphernalia? We could probably forgo selling any other books at all. Shall I dress up in plus fours for the tourists? Do you want to start calling me Billy?"

Nobody called Chris "Billy" or "Billy Moon" anymore. It was a relic, a variation on the name his father had given him when, as a very young boy, Chris had been unable to properly pronounce their surname, and had declared the whole family to be Moons. Over the years all of Chris's childhood nicknames—Billy, CR, and Robin—had fallen to the side. He'd volunteered for service during World War 2, and he'd shaken loose of his childhood, or so he'd hoped.

"Did you let that cat in again?" Abby stood at the top of the stairs in her nightgown with her fingers up to her nose. She was holding back a sneeze.

Was her belly getting bigger? Christopher thought he could just see a difference, a slight curve underneath her billowy silk gown.

"I found the Pooh books," Christopher said.

"You think our customers shouldn't find any part of your father's work in our store?"

"I'm not interested in selling that bear."

"You and your mother have a lot in common." Abby turned away, disappeared around the corner, and Chris returned to the stacks and put three copies of *The House at Pooh Corner* on the shelf. Then he taped up the rest in the box they'd arrived in and wrote out the address for his distributor on a sticky label. He'd send these back.

Christopher opened another box of books and found Dr. Seuss inside. He ran his finger along the spines as he placed the books on the handcart, and then he looked again at *The Cat in the Hat*. He looked at the red-and-white striped top hat, at the umbrella the cat was holding, and the precariously placed fish-bowl, and remembered or realized the truth about the stray cat he'd been feeding and the truth felt odd to him, something like déjà vu.

Hodge was neither a British Shorthair nor a tabby, but a stuffed toy. Abby had purchased a black cat with synthetic fur and straw inside for the nursery, for the boy they were expecting. Hodge was made by Merrythought and Christopher picked him up from the bookshelf where he'd left him.

Chris felt he'd slipped between the cracks. The moment seemed to hold itself up to him for his inspection. Abby had been sneezing, threatening to sneeze, because of this toy?

Christopher looked from the cash register to the front door, examined the spot where Hodge had been scratching, at the muddy paw prints there, and then went to fetch a wet rag. After he'd washed the glass on the door and taken care of the shop's side window he washed out the rag in the kitchen sink, wrung it thoroughly, and hung it on the rack under the sink to dry.

He approached the door again, turned the sign around so that it now read OPEN to passersby.

Hodge was waiting for him by the register. He picked the cat up and turned him over in order to look at the label.

> MERRYTHOUGHT, HYGIENIC TOYS,
> MADE IN ENGLAND.

Chris took the toy cat with him when he made his way up-stairs to ask Abby what she'd meant. He tucked the toy under his arm and started up, taking the first two steps in one go, jumping, and then stopping to get a hold of himself. He would just ask her what she'd meant about the cat, ask what cat she'd been referring to, and that was all, no need to panic.

The bed was still unmade and Abby was at her vanity, she had one of her oversized maternity bras half on, draped over her shoulder but unclasped, and was brushing her auburn hair. When he stepped up to the table and put the toy cat down next to a canister of facial powder, she put the brush down and started tying her hair back into a bun.

"Did you ask after Hodge?"

"Hodge?" she asked.

"Did you ask me if I was feeding the stray cat?"

"Were you?"

This wasn't very helpful so Chris turned Abby to him, away from the mirror, and made her listen to him as he asked it again.

"Did you ask me if I was feeding the cat?"

"Yes. Did you feed him?"

Chris picked the Merrythought toy up from the vanity and held it to her, watched her eyes as she looked it over, checked to see if he might catch some sort of comprehension there.

"This cat?" he asked.

Abby took the toy from him, turned it over in her hands, and then put it down on the vanity and returned to tying back her hair. He waited for a moment, giving her time.

"I'm not sure I understand," she said. "Is there a cat? I mean, is that the cat?"

This was the question Chris wanted to answer, but now that she'd asked aloud the answer seemed further from him. If there was a cat named Hodge how had he come to mistake this toy for him, and if the toy was Hodge then what animal had been eating the table scraps he'd left out? Chris tried to explain the problem to her, he retraced his steps since he'd gotten up, but she was as mystified as he was and suggested that there was nothing for it but to have breakfast.

They had fried eggs, fried mushrooms, potatoes, and more tea. Christopher put jam on wheat toast, but afterwards he couldn't help but bring it up again. It was still relatively early; perhaps they could close for a bit and take a walk? Maybe they could track down the real cat? They might take the trouble to find Hodge and put it to rest.

They took the toy cat with them when they went out. Chris wanted to show the toy around while they looked for Hodge, but the boardwalk along the embankment was still empty. The Butterwalk building was closed but Christopher saw that there were lights on inside and so he went ahead and called "kitty, kitty, kitty" under the fascia. He walked along the line of granite columns, looking behind them and around them hopefully, but he didn't find a real cat there either.

They looked in the windows of the Cherub Pub and Inn. Chris had the impression that the owner, an older man named William Mullett whose family had run the pub for generations, had also taken pity on Hodge over the last few months. He'd seen William feeding Hodge raw halibut from the inn's kitchen, and he wondered why the cat ever ventured over to the Harbour Bookshop given how he made out at the Cherub. They were open for breakfast, so he and Abby ventured in and found William sitting at reception.

"Morning, Christopher," William said. He was a bald and round man who'd been in the first war but otherwise hadn't seen much outside of Dartmouth. "Morning, Abby. What brings you two round this morning? How are the books?"

"Morning, William," Christopher said. He looked at Abby and then back at William and wondered what he wanted to say or ask.

"We've come to ask after a cat," Abby said. "Christopher has had some difficulty with a tabby."

"An English Shorthair," Chris said.

William nodded. "I've been meaning to stop by your shop. There might be a new hardcover I'd be interested in."

"Ah, yes. Well, what brings us in this morning is this stray cat I've seen you feeding. He might be a tabby or an English Shorthair. I called him Hodge."

William considered this. "Ah."

"The question is whether you've seen him. I mean, am I right? Have you been feeding him?"

"That cat?" William asked. He pointed to the toy Chris was still carrying and Chris held the thing up.

"Did you just point to this cat? This one I'm carrying?"

"That's Hodge, isn't it? Yeah?"

"You think this is Hodge?"

William shrugged and then turned to fiddling with a few papers on his desk. He looked down at the list of guests, touched the service bell, and then looked up at them again and nodded. "Yeah, that's Hodge?"

Christopher put the toy down gently in front of William and then turned it over for him so he could see the tag. He leaned over toward the innkeeper and asked him again.

"Are you saying that this toy cat is Hodge? This is the cat you've been feeding?"

William picked the black cat up, turned it over a few times, and then put it back down again. He took a letter opener out of his top drawer and cut the seam in the cat's belly. William pulled out straw.

"No. This can't be him," he said.

Christopher told William that he'd had the same misperception this morning, that he was wondering if there had ever been a cat, and then asked William why he'd cut the toy open.

"Just thought I'd see," William said. "But you're right, Christopher. That's not the cat we know. Did you get that one for the baby?"

Later that afternoon Chris wore his Mackintosh raincoat and his Wellington boots when he left the Harbour Bookshop just to go for a walk. It was around three o'clock in the afternoon, and since there hadn't been a customer since lunch he decided to close the shop early and see where the narrow streets and paths in Dartmouth would take him. He needed to get out into the world, get away from the stale air inside his shop. He'd been confused was all, but a walk would fix that. He would go for a walk and know that what he was seeing in his head matched up with the world outside.

Christopher called "kitty, kitty" just a few times, and when no cat came to him he breathed in and tried to enjoy the moist air as he stood on the boardwalk. He frowned when he looked out at the water and spotted a bit of rubbish floating in the Dart. He'd have to go down to the dock, lean out between a small red leisure sailboat and an old fishing boat that looked like it might rust through, and fetch it out.

It wasn't until he was on the dock and lying on his stomach, halfway eased out over the water, that he wondered if there really was something out there. He stretched until the wet paper wrapper was just within his reach and caught it with his index and middle finger. It was a Munchies candy wrapper, bright red and a bit waxy.

Returning to the shop, Christopher turned the lights on and went to the trash bin behind the front counter. He examined the register to make sure it was locked properly. He wanted to go back out, intended to lock up for the rest of the day, but as he was checking that everything was settled behind the register the front door opened and a customer entered. It was William.

"Afternoon, Christopher."

"William. Glad to see you. Did you remember anything more about that cat?"

"What cat is that, Christopher? The toy cat? No, no. I've come in to look at your books."

William made his way into the stacks, then came over by the register. He moved his lips as he read Eugene Burdick's *The Ugly American* and leaned on the spinner rack.

"Uh, William?"

"Yes, lad?"

"The spinner won't bear up. It's not meant to hold more than books."

There were rules to running a bookstore, rules to being a customer, and sometimes it seemed William didn't understand any of them. A few weeks back he'd come in at two o'clock, found a copy of a book that seemed interesting to him, and spent three hours leaning against the stacks and reading *Charley Weaver's Letters From Mamma*. Now William was going to keep Christopher in the shop for another afternoon of browsing.

He wanted to ask the old man again about Hodge, but he didn't know what to ask. The two of them had made the same mistake, or had had the same hallucination, but how could they talk about it or make sense of it?

While he waited for William to finish up he thought of the Munchies wrapper in the bin. Someone had just tossed their garbage into the Dart. People were losing their grip on the niceties that made life work in Devon. It had something to do with pop music and television. He considered the Munchies wrapper and wondered if it was, in fact, still there. He tried to remember what was on the Munchies label. Something about a crisp at the centre and toffee?

Christopher reached under the register, into the waste bin, and was relieved to pull out the Munchies wrapper. It was still there.

" 'Milk chocolate with soft caramel and crisp biscuit centre,' " he read.

William moved away from the novels to the aisle with popular science books. He thumbed through a guidebook for mushroom identification and then picked up Kinsey's book *Sexual Behavior in the Human Male*.

"That one is for reading at home I think. Would you like it?" He dreaded the idea of old William standing around in the store for hours reading about erections, fellatio, and masochism.

"This fellow died young, didn't he?" William asked.

"Depends on your definitions."

"Can't bring this one home. That would be a scandal. Besides, I wouldn't want the wife reading up on all the ways I was deficient."

"I see. Is there anything then? You'd said there was a book you wanted?"

William looked up at Christopher, a bit surprised. "You're eager to look for Hodge again, Chris?"

Christopher let out a breath and then told William no. He wasn't going anywhere. Then, rather than continue on with that, Christopher held the candy wrapper up in the light and considered it again. He put the candy wrapper back into the trash bin, pushed the bin under the register and out of view, and then took it out again to check the wrapper was still there and still the same. He picked up the trash bin and repeated this several more times. In and out. It was somehow satisfying. He felt reassured each time, back and forth. He felt relieved until it dawned on him what he was doing.

Chris was acting out a scene from one of his father's stories. In the first Pooh book there had been a scene just like this only with a popped balloon and not a Munchies wrapper. In the story the stuffed donkey, Eeyore, had felt better about his ruined birthday once he realized that a deflated balloon could fit inside an empty honey jar. And now, in an effort to prove that he was sane, Christopher was repeating this same simple action.

" 'He was taking the balloon out, and putting it back again, as happy as could be,' " Christopher said.

"What's that?" William asked.

How had Christopher arrived at this? He was reenacting his father's stories in order to convince himself that the world was real?

"Maybe I could find a secret spot for it," William said.

"What's that?"

The old man put Kinsey's book on the counter. And Christopher was struck by something like déjà vu for the second time that day.

The red-and-white cover, the way the words "Based on surveys made by members of the University of the State of Indiana" fit together above the title, it matched the design on the Munchies wrapper. Christopher took the wrapper out of the waste bin and unfolded it on the counter so it was set down flat next to Kinsey's red book.

" 'Milk chocolate with soft caramel and crisp biscuit centre.' " He read the words again.

"What's that?"

Christopher felt some anxiety looking at the juxtaposition, a little like he was underwater and trying to get to the surface. He was not quite drowning, not yet, but air seemed a long way off.

"Nothing," Christopher said.

"Hmmm?"

Christopher took William's money and put the book in a brown paper bag. Then he took the Munchies wrapper out of the waste bin and put it in the cash register just to be sure.

2

While Christopher was coping with toy cats, Munchies wrappers, and Kinsey's report on sexual behavior in the human male, a ten-year-old boy in Paris, a boy named Gerrard Hand, decided that he was dreaming, during a field trip to the police station at Montagne Sainte-Geneviève. He discovered that, in dreams, the past is hidden inside the present. It happened when he was on the third floor of the police museum.

Charles de Gaulle looked down from the glass walls of the police station through painted eyes, and Gerrard could tell that the president knew something. De Gaulle knew the secret, the thing that Papa had done to himself, the thing that neither his mama nor his nana would talk about.

The dozen or so boys and girls from Ménilmontant school stood near the elevators in a chamber separated from the front desk of the police station, from the policemen with their batons and guns, by walls of safety glass. These walls were painted white and displayed life-sized illustrations of civic heroes.

Three of the four figures were generic—a fireman, a policeman, a teacher—but the last figure was Charles de Gaulle.

Gerrard moved to the front of the line, made sure that he was with the first group into the elevator, with the little blond girls whom the teacher liked. His teacher, Mme. Mertfield, made the rest of the boys wait for the second elevator because they had to learn to be quiet and still, but Gerrard stepped into the elevator and was at the first exhibit before there could be any objection.

Gerrard considered the words "Precision, Clarity, Security," the motto that had defined the new role of the police lieutenant in Louis XIV's army. He examined the foppish mannequin dressed in a royal blue uniform with gold trim.

The history of the police and the policing of history began with this: a bicorn or two-cornered hat like the one Napoleon would adopt poised neatly on the head of an army-man dressed in finery. But then Gerrard read about other possible starting points. The police might've started with the establishment of troops to keep the peace in 1521 or in 1224 with Saint Louis' Knights of the Watch. The Knights of the Watch's motto was "He watches so others may rest."

When Gerrard's father had come home from the hospital the first time, Gerrard had resented him. His father had been away for eight months and had become legend to Gerrard, but then when he'd come back to their three-room apartment in the Ménilmontant neighborhood, their daily pattern behind the reinforced concrete walls of the building shifted. For instance, the centre point in the orbit of his mother's attention changed. Pierre would shamble out of the bedroom in his pajamas at random times and Gerrard's mother would bring him medicine and coffee. He had to take pills.

"I'm working on reality," his father said, "but the world won't meet me halfway."

Gerrard's father's curly black hair was always greasy, and he didn't focus but smoked one cigarette after another, knocking ash into his coffee or across his toast with strawberry jam. He'd been a bartender as well as a painter but he said he didn't think he could work again.

"What did they do to you in that hospital?" his mother asked. "When are you going to be a husband to me or a father to your son?"

In the police museum Gerrard admired a glass case displaying brass knuckles and knives of every type: switchblade, ivory handled, serrated. He looked at sharp triangular blades on finger rings, and at a set of hooks and ropes, as the tour guide explained that the police evolved at the same rate of speed as the rest of society. In fact, the tour guide explained that police work and the scientific methods the police employed had pushed the general population toward civilization.

The tour guide led the young students away from the display cases of torture equipment and around the corner to a series of framed photographs. These were set so high on the wall that the children had to crane their necks to see.

"Here we see how the police trained dogs to sniff out criminals and give chase. Notice how these photographs are in a sequence: First the dog discovers the man and forces him out of his hiding place in the wooden shed. Second the police dog chases the man, forcing him to climb to safety, in this case a nearby wood pillar inside the police grounds that gives the criminal a way to elevate himself. But then, behold, the third picture shows the policeman arriving. The policeman whistles to the dog, giving instruction, and the job is complete," the tour guide said.

Gerrard turned away from the sequence and looked at the tour guide. He was a short, thin young man who looked very clean in his thick wool overcoat and with his smartly combed hair. The guide was telling the story of the police, starting over at the beginning, starting with "once upon a time."

The police appeared alongside kings and queens. It began with the absolutes of royalty and torture. Early justice was severe. For instance, criminals were sometimes crushed and pierced in a latticework of hinged spikes, or mauled and hung by their ankles while hooks ripped their flesh, and many more were simply beheaded in the guillotine.

But, Gerrard only found out that he was dreaming, that maybe he was always dreaming whether he was in bed asleep, awake at school, or at the police museum, when he came across the Bertillon system of cataloging and categorizing police photographs. Gerrard examined the faces of criminals from the nineteenth century, and at the details that were used to distinguish the people, one from another. One might have a large nose, another a prominent chin.

He remembered the last day he'd spent with Pierre, with his father. They'd visited the suburb of Neuilly-sur-Seine and a little park on Île de la Grande Jatte. Papa had taken a day off from bartending, he was finally working again, but he'd skipped out to take Gerrard "to see the light on the island." Dressed in a three-piece navy suit and a gray fedora maybe he'd looked a bit like the men in the police photos even without a handlebar mustache or a prominent chin. He'd had the same blank eyes.

When they'd boarded the Metro his father had pointed to

the curved lamps that illuminated the platform, to the spots of reflected light on the tile ceiling above them, and asked Gerrard how long it would take for the train to move away from the light.

Gerrard didn't really understand the question. "How far?" he asked.

Pierre pointed to the curved ceiling above the Metro platform and explained. To move away, from point a to point b, would take forever because there were an infinite number of points in between.

"It's Zeno's paradox. He was a philosopher and he used the example of an arrow in flight instead of a Metro car. He said that an arrow as it takes flight should freeze in place because in any given instant in time an arrow can either move to where it already is, or it can move to where it is not. But it can't move to where it isn't because we're talking about a single instant. So in any given moment there is no movement," his father said.

"How far?"

When they arrived Gerrard squinted and raised his hand to block out the light. His eyes had adjusted to the dimness of the Metro tunnels.

The island was crowded with people, but Gerrard felt there was enough room. There were open spaces between the trees, and there was space between the men in their long beige coats and the women in their high heels and long synthetic skirts. His papa told Gerrard that the strolling day trippers in the park could be and had in fact already been reduced to dots of light, pure color.

His father found a tree to sit under and opened a bottle of Merlot he'd brought along in his briefcase. He drank from it steadily and read from the newspaper *L'Humanité* while Gerrard drifted. Gerrard hid behind trees and pretended to shoot Nazis and Indians.

"Keep an eye out for a woman with an umbrella, or a soldier with a bugle," his papa said. He also told him that after a visit to Île de la Grande Jatte there could be no going back to the regular way Gerrard saw the world. Then he poured more wine.

"May I try a taste, Papa?" Gerrard asked.

There was nothing left but the dregs and Papa sucked those down and then produced two wineglasses and another bottle from his briefcase. Papa lit a cigarette and poured a quarter of a glass of wine for him, but before he gave the cup over Papa took a sip himself, so that the glass was only an eighth of the way full.

Gerrard took a sip. The wine tasted good and he downed the rest in one go. When he stood and wandered in a circle around the maple tree he felt off balance. Through the thick green grass Gerrard spun in circles, holding his arms out to his sides. He spun faster, and then faster still.

"You dizzy yet, son?"

Gerrard stopped spinning and tried to stand perfectly still, but the earth came rushing up at him, at a right angle under his feet, and pulled him off balance. It felt like there was a spring underground that had been released.

Gerrard remembered this as he listened to the tour guide explain how the police gave the children freedom. His father had gone away. No, that wasn't really it. His father was dead, and now he was alone. Gerrard was a little boy who was neither well behaved enough to be admired by adults nor tough and wily enough to be admired by his peers.

Gerrard remembered his father and looked at the exhibits in

the police museum. The tour guide arranged the children in a line so they could get their pictures taken. He explained that Alphonse Bertillon had developed a method of filing mug shots, a system of measuring facial features, and a method for photographing crime scenes.

"Bertillon changed the way police work was done in the twentieth century," the tour guide said. He grabbed a wooden stool and dragged it alongside the accordion lens of the special camera and then set it down in front. This was where the children were to sit.

Gerrard was at the back of the line next to a wax reproduction of Henri-Jacques Pranzini's decapitated head. In 1888 Pranzini had been convicted of the murder of three young women and put to death by guillotine. Gerrard felt a coldness on his back and in his stomach as he glanced nervously at the wax head and read the placard on the display case.

Pranzini had gained his victims' confidence by posing as a doctor.

On the island his father had poured Gerrard another glass of wine after the first one and then made him settle down in the grass and sit still so he could listen to a story.

"You've been working on your English?" he asked.

"Mama says I don't have to learn it yet."

"You should learn to speak English."

"Yes, Papa."

"I won't be around to help you later. You'll have to do a lot, everything, on your own. But now, today, I'll help you. There are a lot of good stories in English, and this is one of them."

The House at Pooh Corner didn't start with an introduction but with a contradiction, because it was the second Pooh book and so there was no need for another introduction, because when they asked the animals in the stories what the opposite of an introduction was they were told that it was, of course, just a contradiction. Also the second Pooh book started with a contradiction because it turned out that the very best Pooh stories were the ones that were dreamed up by Christopher Robin when he was sleeping, dreamed up while Pooh, his stuffed bear, sat by his bed thinking grand thoughts about nothing, but Christopher Robin could never remember any of those.

"One day when Pooh was walking in the Forest, there were one hundred and seven cows on a gate . . ." No, you see, we have lost it. It was the best, I think. Well, here are some of the other ones, all that we shall remember now. But, of course, it isn't really Good-bye, because the Forest will always be there . . . and anybody who is Friendly with Bears can find it.

Gerrard leaned against the tree while his father read aloud, first in English and then, translating as he read, in French.

In the police museum, one of the noisy boys, a freckled kid with brown hair and a sly grin, sat on the wooden stool as the tour guide continued on about fingerprints and surveillance. The tour guide put his finger in the air to interrupt himself, ducked beneath the dark cloth, and the boy smiled as the camera flashed. Next the tour guide removed the negative from the back of the camera and loaded another.

The Forest was always there waiting for him because every story started with a contradiction. Gerrard took a step forward as one of the good little blond girls took her place on the stool, but when she got down and another boy, a neat and tidy good one in a nice red bow tie and grey jacket, climbed up on the stool to have his picture taken, Gerrard found he was stuck. If every story started with a contradiction then maybe there wasn't really a floor or a police museum.

Gerrard's feet sank into the floor. He looked down and saw that the hard wood had been replaced, there wasn't any hard wood beneath him but just soft mud, and Gerrard got down on his hands and knees to examine this difference. He stuck his fingers in, and the surface gave. He sat down and put both his hands in the mud.

"Stand up, Gerrard. You're blocking the way," Mme. Mertfield said. He looked at her with her brown hair pulled back and her bifocals and felt glad to be in trouble. "You have to get out of the way now," she said. She thought he was a good one too, he could tell, but maybe he'd disappoint her.

"You can't just sit there," Mme. Mertfield said.

She was right. Instead of just sitting there by himself Gerrard leaned over and whispered in the ear of one of the good girls. Her name was Louise. All Gerrard knew about her was that she wore very thick glasses—he'd tried them on once and could barely see through them—and that she could kick very hard if she wanted. He whispered that Albert said they shouldn't get their pictures taken. Albert was just another one of the boys in class, but invoking his name had been enough. Louise smiled as she nodded to him, and then sat down too.

"Now children, don't you want to get your picture taken?" Mme. Mertfield asked.

"No, Madame. I do not wish for my photograph to be taken," Gerrard said.

"We don't want our pictures taken," Louise said and giggled.

Samuel sat down next, and then Philippe joined him, sitting in line. He was the boy who had already had his photo taken.

"Who is next?" the tour guide asked and turned to find most of the children sitting down on the floor.

"Children, you must all get up now," Mme. Mertfield said.

Lucie Melancon, a young woman who was killed on a street-car, murdered, and then left to be found at the next stop, a woman remembered only for her mysterious demise, smiled at Gerrard from her newsprint portrait. Her blond bob and blue eyes were rendered in greyscale but evident despite this.

"Children, you must get up so that our tour can continue," Mme. Mertfield said. She turned to Gerrard; she was not smiling. "Gerrard, come with me."

She took him by the elbow and forced him up and out. She was a remarkably strong woman, but Gerrard could see that she was sweating as she clamped down on his arm with one hand and pressed the button for the elevator with the other.

"I don't know what kind of adventure you think you're on," Mme. Mertfield said, "but I won't tolerate this disruption."

When the elevator doors opened Gerrard looked over his shoulder and caught sight of the tour guide as he paced back and forth in the mud. One boy stood up and the tour guide approached him, asking him to please get up on the stool for his picture and wouldn't his mother like to get a photo of her handsome son, but the boy shook his head no. He reached out for the guide and put his muddy hand on the guide's clean wool jacket leaving a handprint there, and then sat down again. Then another student stood up on the other side. The tour guide turned to her and paced over in her direction, and the exhortations and pleading began again.

Mme. Mertfield dragged Gerrard into the elevator, pressed the button, and then stepped back into the museum when the doors started to close. "Go and wait by the front desk," she said. "Tell the policeman what you've done."

When the elevator doors closed Gerrard remembered his father again.

Papa shook his son by his foot, and Gerrard opened his eyes and laughed. "Are you paying attention?" his father asked.

Then Gerrard was on the bottom floor, back with the fireman, the teacher, the policeman, and Charles de Gaulle. He looked at the painted figures from inside the elevator, but he didn't move, and before long the elevator doors closed again. Inside the elevator Gerrard waited for someone, probably his teacher, to push the button and bring him back up again.

3

In July of 1961 Christopher found a poster on the Harbour's bulletin board, a poster that didn't belong there. What gave it away was that it was attached with paste rather than the tacks Chris provided. This, along with the poster's French slogan and the title card and explanation—the silk screen poster was entitled "Pooh Attacks the Police" and the cartoon bear was apparently either a symbol or mascot for striking workers in a future Paris—marked the poster as out of place. According to the title card tacked underneath, it was a poster from the future, set to be printed seven years hence, in 1968.

Chris noticed the orange rectangle as he wheeled in a shipment of new books on his handcart, but he didn't stop to look at it at first. Instead he unpacked boxes and shelved the books by category and in alphabetical order. He used his pocketknife to cut the tape on the first box. The blade was rusty and dull after years of use on Cotchford Farm and passage through a world war, but it was still sharp enough to cut, and he opened a box containing a dozen copies of J. M. Barrie's *Peter Pan*.

Barrie had been one of his father's friends. Finding the right shelf Chris recalled how proud his father had been to help Barrie by funding one of his Peter Pan stage productions, but Chris didn't see how the two of them had much in common. Barrie romanticized childhood and elevated fantasy while Chris's father stood back from both in order to expose how these things were absurd. Chris's father was just having a bit of fun even if many readers didn't get the joke.

Later his father admitted to it. He wrote his autobiography and directly spoke about the narcissism of children, but this was ignored. Critics and readers continued to insist that the Pooh stories and his father's poems were somehow part of a general celebration of childhood. Certainly his father had not made his fortune because readers saw and enjoyed his cynicism.

On the other hand, Barrie and Christopher's father really did share some basic assumptions. After all, it took a hundred years to invent the bourgeois notion of childhood, and Barrie and Chris's father helped along these lines. Before Peter Pan and Pooh, books written for children taught practical skills, but what with electricity and so many cogs and wheels children's work was no longer necessary. Once children didn't have to play a role in the economy they became something like a special type of pet, and their funny ways, their cute imaginations, their fantasy worlds and delusions—all of these things were to be indulged.

The difference between Barrie and his father was that Barrie envied children. Barrie couldn't quite stand up to the pressures of modern life, couldn't hold up under the strain. For him, retreating into a permanent childhood, a fantasy, was an appealing prospect, but Chris's father was made of stronger stuff.

Chris looked at the poster but still didn't see it as strange, a monochrome print of the silhouette of a bear encircled by three police officers. They were clearly French police officers, marked as such by the brims of their kepis as shown in negative space. Chris didn't read the French words along the bottom but just saw they were there.

Vous ne récupérera pas cet ours dans son cage.

Christopher cut the tape on another box. And found a new book, something by Dr. Seuss, inside the box. Seuss's title was a simple rhyme.

"*The Cat in the Hat.*" Chris spoke the title aloud.

It made sense; the trends fit together. Christopher's childhood had been made possible by the technologies developed during the First World War. The Erector Set, the cellophane zoo animals, everything except for Pooh himself had been brand new. The teddy bear craze had come with the American president Theodore Roosevelt, but after the Great War there were even more of these mass-produced childhood fantasies. After the war there'd been a flood of celluloid dolls and Kodak cameras.

Vous ne récupérera pas cet ours dans son cage. That translated into something like "You will not put the bear back in his cage."

Christopher put down the box of Dr. Seuss books and approached his bulletin board. The poster was about 48 by 69 centimeters and had been pasted over a notice for piano lessons and an advert for A. J. Cronin's *The Judas Tree.* Chris put out his hand and touched the edge of the notice, where it met the bulletin board, and wondered how it could have come to be in his shop. He tried to pull it down, but the paste held it fast and rather than come down the paper started to tear.

When Abby came downstairs she wasn't much help. "Why is the card in English while the poster is in French?" Christopher asked. "And how would something from an auction end up in my shop? That's where this is from. See, at the bottom it says 'Christie's, London.'"

"Sometimes in order to be realistic you have to accept the impossible," Abby said. She fetched her iron and a spray bottle and they set to work on steaming the poster off the bulletin board.

"How many times is this going to happen?" Christopher said. "I think something's gone wrong. Something has broken somewhere, and this is the result."

Christopher took the bulletin board upstairs. He opened his cardboard box, the one he kept in the coat closet. Instead of books there was a stuffed cat made by Merrythought, a Munchies wrapper, a copy of Françoise Sagan's *Bonjour Tristesse,* and a jam jar full of mud inside. And, as soon as they could peel it from the bulletin board, Christopher would put the poster in there as well.

"Here," Abby said. "I think it's coming loose."

Daniel was standing up in his crib when Christopher brought the stuffed cat in. He was smack dab in the middle of the mattress, standing there so that the mobile dangled down around his little head. A plastic aeroplane with a bright red propeller was resting against his left cheek and an orange moon was covering his right eye, but Daniel didn't appear to notice. Christopher leaned over the bars of the crib, but the boy was out of reach. He whistled to his son. He tapped the bars with his knuckle and called out to him.

"Daniel," he said. "What are you doing? Found a good spot to get your legs under you? Thinking about walking?"

Daniel didn't respond to Chris but just watched his own

hands as he raised them to his face. Daniel stared past the plastic toys on strings. He flitted his fingers through the air and made a gurgling noise.

Raising a son was different for Christopher than it had been for his own father. When Chris wasn't secreting away anomalies around the bookshop he was expected to be involved in ways that his father never was. Daniel's toilet training, for instance, was something that required thought, preparation, and discussion. Abby had ordered a good half-dozen different books on parenting and she'd asked Chris to read along. He'd tried Dr. Spock's book and A. S. Neill's *Summerhill*.

They advocated a kind of humanistic approach that Christopher found very difficult to argue against, but now that his son was nearly a year old Christopher was deciding these authors might not be relevant. Quite apart from the contemporary problem of guiding a child without using force or the problem of not interfering with his natural development, something was wrong here. Daniel wasn't human in the way these humanists required. He refused to lie down or sit; now that he could stand the boy always stood. And if Christopher were to pick Daniel up, try to hold the tot in his arms, the experience would be something like picking up a column or piece of lumber. Chris could pick Daniel up, but Daniel would just go on standing.

Still, the boy looked just like him. This was his son. They kept his hair short and dressed Daniel in modern jumpers or footsie pajamas and never in britches and knee socks, but to look at Daniel was to see himself, his own storybook image. It was impossible to miss the resemblance.

Christopher took the Merrythought cat, a cat no longer called Hodge, and held it out for his son to look at, but he couldn't get Daniel's attention. Chris ran his finger along the seam on the cat's belly, fingered the red thread Abby had used to sew the animal up after William's experiment, and wished he'd left the thing in the box.

One reason Christopher couldn't argue with Dr. Spock or *Summerhill* was because their humanism was his own. It was something Christopher had inherited along with the stuffed bear. Maybe his father's version was different from the radical variety held in esteem by A. S. Neill, but there was common ground. His father and *Summerhill* thought that, even without God, there were human beings. There would always be human beings and a coherent world for them to live in. Standing there with Hodge, moving the animal back and forth and failing to get his son's attention, Christopher wasn't so sure.

He tried again with another toy, a blue dog. This one was less appealing than Hodge; the dog was too stiff and stood in an unnatural way. It was run through with wires in order to hold it in an active pose, but it was also less unsettling for Christopher to touch. The blue dog toy was meant to exactly replicate a television character, and this gave it some sort of real basis.

Chris held Huckleberry Hound out to his son. "Look, Daniel. You have a friend." Christopher shook the toy but failed to bring it to life.

Would Daniel ever develop a relationship with these objects? Could he do that? The truth about Pooh was that the stuffed bear had really belonged to Christopher. He remembered picking it out at the toy store from a row of identical silly bears. Christopher's Pooh had had an especially pleading look in his glass eyes. That bear had sort of called out to him from the shelf in the toy store.

"Yes, please. I'll take that one," he'd said.

Pooh had made the transition from a shelf in the toy store to a shelf in Chris's nursery and then, over a few weeks, the bear had come to life. The fact that his father had taken this life and used it, that his father had moved Christopher himself onto the pages of his fictions, didn't negate the fact that Christopher had once held a stuffed bear with real affection. Christopher had once given a personality to something lifeless—to an object. Why did he have such trouble detecting a personality in his son?

Daniel turned around in his crib but did not look at his father. He almost seemed to intentionally look away. Although that couldn't be right.

Chris shook the cartoon character again. "I'm a TV dog. Aren't I, Daniel? I live on television?"

Daniel stood in his crib with his head draped in the plastic toys from his mobile. He let his hands drop to his side. Christopher watched to see what would happen next. He wondered what his father might write about such a moment.

As a little boy Christopher had always been mostly content to be a character in his father's books. He'd quite liked being the famous Christopher Robin, receiving stuffed animals and other toys in the mail from acquaintances and strangers, and always being at the centre of some imaginary world. He remembered being delighted by an oversized stuffed piglet he'd received at the age of eight and then being rather disappointed in a red rubber ball that arrived in the post that same day. Had it been his birthday?

"Daniel, I'm your toy dog," Christopher said. "Woof. Woof. Woof."

Sitting with his son, sitting in the boy's nursery with his memories of Pooh and holding the boy's blue dog, Chris felt quite absurd.

His own father had been more confident. So confident that he hadn't made rules but rather suggestions.

Once his father told him that one mustn't hold one's knife and fork vertically between bites but should place them in a horizontal position; Chris had asked why. His father, who never wanted to rely on mere authority or tradition, had cooked up a reason.

"What if the ceiling should give way and someone should fall on the dining table? If you're holding your fork vertically the person might be impaled while you're having pudding," his father said.

Christopher generally ate his pudding with a spoon. Also he thought it was unlikely that the ceiling should collapse during dinner in the way his father described, but he obeyed after that. He always replaced his cutlery on each side of his plate between bites. His father had power even when he was absurd, but now Christopher was the father and there was nobody there for Chris to convince.

Christopher spoke, and he made the boy's TV dog dance, but there was no response inside the nursery.

4

Gerrard had difficulty focusing on the repetitious conjuga-
tions he was asked to perform on his chalkboard. All the
other students wrote how to be in the past, in the present, and in
the future, but Gerrard looked up at the ceiling, put his chalk
down, and wondered how it might be possible to get a firm grip
on tense.

Was. Is. Will be.

Gerrard stared at the ceiling and did not see that the teacher
was looking at him. The lady was frowning at him, calling his
name, but Gerrard did not hear. It was not until she approached
him, leaned down, and put her jowly face in between Gerrard
and the place where the paint was flaking away on the ceiling,
it wasn't until he could smell the mix of mothballs and roses that
clung to Mme. Mertfield that Gerrard realized he was in trouble.

"Monsieur Hand, there is no sleeping allowed in this class. If
you are not interested in learning then you should simply stay
home."

"I was not sleeping, madame," Gerrard said.

"No? What is the conditional form?"

Gerrard paused and tried to find the words to explain it to her.

"If you don't pay attention you will not learn," the teacher said.

"Yes, madame. That's right."

"You agree?"

"It's conditional."

She took Gerrard by his shirt collar and marched him to the front of the class. She asked Gerrard to stand in the corner with his face toward the wall, instructed the boy to push his nose against the wall, to stand extra close. Gerrard did as he was told. He stood perfectly still, with his nose smashed against the wall, and wondered how he knew the wall would stay. After all, he could push very hard.

After school Gerrard had settled in to look at the pictures in the latest *Tintin* when his mother and her new boyfriend Patrick arrived. They made noise in the stairway, laughing and shouting, and a sinking feeling took hold of Gerrard. Patrick was going to stay the night. Gerrard knew it right in the middle of his stomach.

"How was school, Gerrard?" Patrick asked.

"Fine, sir."

Patrick stood in the doorway and blinked.

"Hello, little one," his mother said. She was wearing dark red lipstick and had her hair pulled back in a bun. Usually she wore her hair down and went without makeup on days when she had to work. She said it didn't matter if she got made up or not, that there was always another girl behind another desk for the boss to look at. There were a hundred girls on her floor, all of them typing on IBM electrics, and, according to her, all of them more presentable than his mother usually was. She would be the only one wearing slacks, but not on the days that she was going to see Patrick. His mother was still dressed casually, but to Gerrard the black skirt and grey turtleneck seemed wrong on her. It would have been better if she'd just gone ahead and dressed up in something formal, like the other mothers Gerrard knew, rather than this way, like a yé-yé girl.

"Hello, Mama," Gerrard said.

"Patrick is staying for dinner."

Patrick just stared at Gerrard, and Gerrard closed his comic book and went straight to the divan. Patrick took off his trench coat and folded it in half, then took off his tie and folded that. He placed these on the table, next to Gerrard's plate, and then headed for the kitchen while Gerrard's mother picked up the jacket and tie and hung them up properly in the hall closet.

"Where is the wine?" Patrick asked from the other room.

Gerrard looked out over the rooftops at the Eiffel Tower, at the chimneys, antennas, and soot. Outside the buildings and the sky were both the color of limestone. As Gerrard lay down on the sofa and stared at the high ceiling he listened to his mother move dishes around in the kitchen.

Later, after dinner, Gerrard asked if he could stay up to listen to Europe 1, to the bebop jazz they played after seven. Rather than answer him herself, Gerrard's mother looked at Patrick.

Patrick told Gerrard's mother that he'd take care of bedtime. He grabbed Gerrard around the waist, and before Gerrard could object, he carried him to his bedroom, placed him on his bed, told him to strip down and go to sleep.

"Do you like Bud Powell?" Gerrard said.

"Strip."

"I'm not tired."

Gerrard reassured himself that in a few minutes he would

simply get up off the bed and leave. The lock on his bedroom
door did not work because the mechanism was jammed. All he
had to do was wait for his mother and her friend to go to her
room, and then sneak back to the kitchen where Billie Holiday
would be singing "Let's Call the Whole Thing Off." He waited
what seemed like a long time, but what might have been only a
few minutes, before lightly stepping out of bed. When Gerrard
tried the door he found that it wouldn't open. Patrick was outside the door, in the dark, holding it closed, and Patrick was
stronger than Gerrard.

"Let me out," Gerrard said.

Patrick didn't budge. Gerrard pulled and pulled on the door,
but the door did not open. Finally, after trying and trying again,
Gerrard lay down on the bed determined to wait it out. Patrick
had to go away sometime.

Gerrard dreamed that the ground beneath his feet was made of
soft grey clay. Gerrard made an indentation, the beginnings of
a trench, as he walked a tight circle around a metal pole. When
he looked to the horizon he saw that there was light, but there
was no source for it. The sky was a matte painting—it didn't just
look like a painting; he could see it really was a painting—a
lighter shade of grey than the ground, but that was all. He
touched the metal spindle, looked at his loafers, and then out at
the horizon again. It was nothing but a screen, and he thought
about walking up to the sky and punching his hand through it.

In the way that often happens in dreams, the scene shifted.
Gerrard was in the city. The clay beneath his feet hardened
into . . . Paris. He was standing on cobblestones. The metal
spindle was gone, replaced by an elephant made of stone and

run through by a spiral staircase. The staircase pierced the elephant's belly, and if he'd wanted he could have climbed in through the hole in the elephant's stone stomach. Rainwater poured from the elephant's trunk.

The elephant sat in the centre of a roundabout. Narrow avenues led away to each point on the compass. On one of these narrow streets, perhaps eleven meters away, a glamorous woman was sitting at a café table. From a distance she looked like the actress Simone Signoret. She held up a pastis glass and the orange color of her Ricard reflected in the sunlight of the early afternoon. She saw Gerrard and waved at him, gesturing for him to approach.

As he sat down she asked, "Do you know where you are?" She pushed a bulbous glass bottle of orange soda to him. He unscrewed the cap and then paused, nervous of taking a sip. Instead of Simone Signoret the dream woman now looked like his mother, only her hair was a darker shade of brown, and her skin was a bit darker. She looked like his mother only younger and more beautiful. She was a dream.

"You're precocious," the woman said and brought her Ricard up to toast him. She drank. "You think you can tell the difference between being awake and dreaming already?"

Gerrard took a sip of his drink, but it was watery and weak. He looked inside the bottle and saw the orange pulp had settled at the bottom. He screwed the cap back on and shook the bottle, watched the sugar water and bits of orange and nectarine mix, then unscrewed the cap and took a quick sip. That was better.

"You're not my mama," Gerrard said. He drank from the bottle and then tried to set it back on the table, but the table was grooved. Pictures of animals—of snakes and ducks and lizards and owls and more—were engraved into the uneven surface of the stone tabletop. Gerrard put his bottle down slowly, carefully, but it tipped and spilled anyway. The liquid sloshed out.

"It's true. I'm not your mama," the woman said. She was smiling in a condescending way, like she was laughing at him. She reached over and set his bottle right.

His dream mother stood up. She was stunning and strange in her red silk dress with black polka dots, with her aura of celebrity, but still she went into the café to fetch a dish towel. She left Gerrard sitting outside by himself. He looked up and down the street and worried that he heard footsteps. He knew he was dreaming, but he wasn't sure if there would be monsters in the dream or not.

Gerrard sat in the sun on the cramped avenue, in an old part of Paris where the streets were narrow and dirty, a part of Paris that smelled of dirt and cigarette smoke. Gerrard took another swig from his bottle, swallowed the carbonated liquid in the wrong way, and started coughing and sputtering.

If it was all a dream, why couldn't he stop coughing? Were his worries bringing on exactly what he feared most? He decided to think of something else, but even when he quit coughing he could still hear footsteps. He listened to them get louder.

The woman in the red dress put down a white dish towel with green stripes that reminded Gerrard of snakes on the spot where he'd spilled his orange drink. He saw her arm and the towel before he realized she'd returned. He was startled.

"I don't want to see him," Gerrard said.

"Who?"

"I don't want to see Papa right now," he said. "He's dead. I don't want to see him dead."

"What if it wasn't your real father, but your mother's friend? What if you could do something about him? Isn't that why you came here?" She wiped the table with the dish towel, soaking up the sugar water that had pooled around the owl, the kangaroo, and the snake.

Gerrard did want to do something about his mother's friend. Before he could think of just what that might be his dream mother reached under the table and brought out some stuffed animals. She placed a stuffed bear, tiger, kangaroo, and a little stuffed donkey on the table where the spill had been.

"Gerrard, do you know where you are?" she asked.

"I'm in the dream," he said.

"And do you know who I am?"

"You're my mother. You're my mama after all," he said.

She took him by his hand and looked at him. She looked Gerrard in the eye and told him that she wasn't exactly his mother, but he could call her that and it would be fine. "Let's talk about your animals," she said. "Your father told you about them, didn't he. He read to you about your animals from a book?"

"Not my animals. They're Christopher's animals."

The animals on the table were threadbare and old. The yellow bear's button eyes dangled from strings, and the donkey had spots where his grey fur had been rubbed away. The woman who was not Gerrard's mother picked the animals up again and put them back in her cloth purse. She finished her wine and then asked Gerrard if he was finished with his orange soda. Gerrard nodded yes.

"Let's go for a walk."

The woman in the red dress led Gerrard back down the narrow street. They squeezed between the limestone walls and made their way toward the elephant building. Gerrard thought it might be a Heffalump and that he didn't want to go inside or up the stairs. Gerrard remembered the animals that had been carved into the table, the way the grooves felt, and he wished that he'd drunk all of his orange soda when he'd had a chance. He squeezed through from Paris back to the flat grey circle where he'd been before, ending up not at an elephant building but back at the metal pole. Back on the damp and giving clay, Gerrard was thirsty.

"You remember where you are?"

"I'm nowhere," Gerrard said.

"It hasn't changed. You told me before."

"I'm in the dream."

She took the animals out of her cloth bag and put them down in the clay. Then she dragged the bear and the pig across the surface, pushing hard enough so that the clay moved. Pushing the stuffed animals along, she made ruts in the clay. She was digging with them.

"You want the tiger?" the woman asked.

"I don't know. Won't they get dirty that way?"

The woman held up the stuffed animals to him and he saw that they were spotless. If anything they were now in better condition, a little less threadbare than they'd been. The bear's eyes were tightly sewn in place; the donkey and kangaroo seemed to have more fur.

Gerrard used the donkey to mark the earth. He pushed the small animal against the ground and dug a hole using the donkey's head. He piled up the clay into a hill. The woman used the bear to make a figure eight in the clay, and then together they both dug a trench around the pole, using each animal to mark the spot.

"Are you dead?" Gerrard asked the woman. He didn't know why he asked. It had something to do with the digging, and the weight of the stuffed donkey in his hands.

The woman said nothing, but she reached out and touched Gerrard's cheek. She had clay on her hand, wet clay that stuck to him, and Gerrard pulled back.

"Am I dead too?"

"No."

"Why am I not dead?"

"You haven't lived long enough."

"I don't want to die," Gerrard said.

Gerrard thought about how everybody died, how everybody was fragile. Even his real mother, even her friend, they were neither of them so big that they couldn't get hurt or die. His mother especially was small. She was always getting sick, telling him about what hurt and where it hurt, but even her friend could be hurt. He'd seen it. His mother's friend had shown Gerrard a wound on his shin, right below the knee. A three-millimeter gash, a straight line below the knee. His mother's friend had been trying to climb a fence and cut himself when he fell onto a street sign. The edge caught him on the leg.

Gerrard had been awake when he'd admired the wound. It was a real wound, and Gerrard had asked to see it again and again. He was impressed that her mother's friend didn't cry, but even more impressed to see him wounded. Gerrard asked to hear the story of how it had happened, how he'd gotten the cut. It didn't make any sense. His mother's friend had been climbing a fence in the sixth Arrondissement, a fence around the hotel where he worked, and he admitted he'd been drunk. Why was he on the fence? Why was he drunk at work?

"It was late. Long after we'd gotten off for the night."

"Why did you go back?"

"It was late."

"Why were you on the fence?"

The answers never came and his mother's friend pulled his pant leg down over the wound.

Gerrard felt better. Looking at the blank grey earth, at the grey screen that had replaced the sky, he felt as though he was making something.

5

Gerrard's mother looked young and scared as they sat in the hall outside Patrick's hospital room in Hôtel-Dieu. She was nervous being there and responded to every request the staff people made. They were sitting in wooden chairs against the rubber strip set into the plaster to protect the wall from wayward gurneys. The infection in Patrick's leg had spread, and now his mother's friend had a blood infection. The doctors had given him drugs to make him sleep and slipped a mask over his face to help him breathe.

Patrick wasn't threatening anymore; he wasn't the big man he'd been, but had shrunk. The unconscious body under the stiff hospital sheets was a fragile thing, and Gerrard felt bad for it. He wished Patrick would wake up so that Gerrard could say he was sorry. He hadn't really meant it.

Gerrard and his mother were asked to wait in the hall and, since Gerrard's mother was not married to Patrick, the two of them were viewed with suspicion by the nurses. It was late at night, much later than Gerrard was usually allowed to stay up.

The hospital had a strange smell. There were a variety of machines to see and old men and women were occasionally wheeled by on their way from a procedure to bed, or from bed to a procedure. There was fear in their eyes, and Gerrard felt a certain amount of pity for them, but in a detached way.

Gerrard felt a bit guilty for his curiosity. Were the bruises on the old lady's arms a symptom of her illness? Was the old man with thin grey hair that stuck out in all directions and who was wearing a sunflower patterned gown muttering obscenities because he was scared, or were his words a symptom of his disease?

Gerrard's mother looked at herself in her compact mirror, adjusted her lipstick, put the mirror away, and then took it out again and looked at her cheeks. She took out a piece of tissue paper from her purse and wiped the rouge from her face and patted at her lips in an effort to remove the red color there. She didn't want to look pretty after all. She looked at herself in her little mirror and thought it over again, turned the bottom of the tube of lipstick, and then turned the tube the other way. She couldn't decide.

"This is the hospital where you were born," she said. "I gave birth to you here."

Gerrard didn't know what to say, didn't particularly like being reminded of being an infant. He wasn't curious about the circumstances of his birth, but he did want to know about the hospital, about how it worked. "Did it hurt?" he asked.

His mother smiled a thin smile, her soft face tightening, and her partially red lips pressing into a slightly curved line. "I don't remember if it hurt," she said. "They gave me drugs to make me sleep and forget."

"What kind of drugs?"

"I don't remember the names, but they told me. Pain drugs partially."

"Did they stick you with needles or give you pills?"

"They injected the drug, or one of the drugs. I think they gave me pills too. I remember they wheeled me around on one of those gurneys and I saw strange things."

His mother described a machine the size of a small room. They were keeping the children who had polio inside the machine, and it was breathing for them. Four children were stowed in the machine, with their heads outside and propped on shelves attached to the machine. The children were sleeping and the machine made a sound like a vacuum cleaner.

She said that she'd thought the children in the machine were dead. She worried that the nurse had killed them, but then she'd remembered how the doctor had warned her about the hallucinations and paranoia the drugs might cause.

"The drugs made it hard to think. I remember the wall of the breathing machine, and I remember waking up to find you were already born."

"Did Papa stay here when he was sick?"

Gerrard's mother went back to adjusting her makeup, licking her lips and holding up the compact mirror to the light.

Gerrard watched as a man in a white lab coat walked past rolling a tray that contained knives and scalpels, and a basin of dark fluid.

"He was on a different floor. I hate this place," his mother said.

Gerrard got up from the chair and walked the length of the hallway. He found an open door and stepped inside the empty hospital room. It smelled like bleach and dust burning on a warm radiator. The dark wood floors were scuffed from metal wheels and the blue cotton curtains on the windows had faded in the sun.

He left the empty hospital room and moved on to explore what was behind the next door. There the walls were lined with light blue tile that reminded him of a swimming pool. It was an operating room. Knives and rubber gloves, basins and paper aprons were set out on a table. Gerrard stepped inside, stood in the middle of the room, put his hands on the pillow, on the spot where the patient's head would go, and thought about blood and internal organs. He listened to his heartbeat, realized that his stomach was empty, and wondered if he needed to pee yet. He stopped and felt his body working, all his parts sloshing along, working together.

"What are you doing in here, boy?" the nurse asked. She had a friendly face, not exactly pretty but not mean. Her hair was pulled back into a bun and she was wearing round wire-rimmed glasses. She reached out to Gerrard, took him by the elbow, and escorted him toward the door before Gerrard had a chance to answer.

"Did you touch anything?" she asked. Gerrard was back in the hallway before he could answer.

"I didn't touch anything except the pillow, madame," he said.

The nurse shut the door behind them, and then turned and looked Gerrard up and down, appraisingly.

"Where are your parents?" she asked.

The nurse escorted Gerrard back to his mother. She was sitting in the same spot, apparently not having noticed Gerrard had gone. She was still looking at herself in her mirror. When the nurse cleared her throat she didn't look up, but simply nodded at her own reflection.

"Thank you, mademoiselle," his mother said.

"I found him in an operating room that was to be kept sterile."

"Did you touch anything?" his mother asked.

"No."

"He didn't touch anything," his mother said.

"Please keep track of your child, madame," the nurse said.

"Of course. Thank you."

When the nurse left, his mother put away her mirror and looked up at Gerrard. She looked tired and faded, but confident. She told him that they were going to leave the hospital, that they'd spent enough time there, more than enough, and that they were going home.

"I'm sorry, Mama. I didn't mean to make it so we had to leave."

His mother stood up and put her arms around her son, gave him a brief hug. She looked him in the eye and told him not to worry, that it was not his fault. They were not leaving because of anything he'd done.

On their way to the exit Gerrard's mother stopped at the nurses' station and asked if Patrick had woken up yet. He had not.

"Would you tell him that we waited for him? Would you tell him that we hope he feels better soon?"

"I'm sorry, Mama," Gerrard said.

"It's not your fault," she said.

But Gerrard didn't believe her. They wouldn't see Patrick again. Even if Patrick were to get better, they were leaving him behind for good. Gerrard didn't quite know why he thought this was true, but as they walked down the hall toward the stairway, made their way past another frightened old lady with tubes in her nose and a vacant stare, he stopped and made as if to tie his shoes. He got down on his hands, squatted so that he could put his palm down on the hard wood floor, and found that the floor was soft. It had a give to it that he wouldn't have expected. Gerrard scratched with his index finger and the wood broke apart. The soft wood came up and he held it in his hand.

Hiding the soft wood away in his jacket pocket was easy. His mother never noticed this sort of thing. He doubted she'd see what was happening beneath their feet even if he pointed it out to her.

When they were on the street Gerrard felt his feet sink into soft cobblestones. Each step required more effort, and it wasn't until they were on the Metro, until he leaned up against his mother and closed his eyes, that he came back to himself. The world was out there, beyond his eyelids. Everything was real and solid again as he listened to the rhythmic clacking of the Metro.

His mother put her arm around him and Gerrard drifted into sleep.

6

Christopher wished the doctor's office was cleaner. Had no one in Brixham heard of the pathogenic theory or Pasteur? Doctor Reinhard's rolltop mahogany desk was littered with a glass ashtray full of cigarette butts, papers, and what appeared to be black-and-white pebbles. The dark orange wallpaper had an aura of the nineteenth century clinging to it.

The doctor didn't seem to notice or care how his sloppiness affected Daniel, or how difficult it was for Daniel to endure strange and disordered spaces. If the office had been hygienic and functional then maybe the news wouldn't have cut so deep. It would have seemed objective rather than personal. As it was, when the doctor told him that Daniel was mentally deficient Chris felt like he'd been punched.

"When you described Daniel's hand flapping, his rigidity and lack of age-appropriate bonding, it seemed likely the boy was what we call self-isolating or non-normative," the doctor said. "The testing I performed confirmed this diagnosis."

The doctor could use euphemisms, but he couldn't compensate for the inappropriate tangibility of the office, of his person. It was too late. Simply by allowing the physical aspects of his life to be so visible the doctor had already intruded. The doctor was standing too close to him. Chris could feel the man's damp breath on his face and smell it clinging to the air. Chris stepped back.

Abby stood dumbly by the office door, her arms draped across Daniel's small frame. The two of them looked blank, uncomprehending, Abby with her permanent curls, her lipstick, her copper-colored dress and red scarf, and Daniel with his eyes that never seemed to focus, with his knee pants and a bow tie, but who might as well have been wearing pajamas or a hospital gown.

There was something incomprehensible about the moment. The doctor was telling them that they should feed Daniel more bananas, that his diet was very important.

Daniel was autistic. It was a disease brought about by the deficiencies in their family. His symptoms were brought on by their unconscious neglect.

Usually it was the mother who was at fault, the doctor said, but not always. The doctor puffed on his pipe and then held up a banana and a leaflet. He offered these items to Christopher. Then the doctor reached under the desk and produced a plastic dollhouse. He set the toy down next to the glass ashtray and asked Christopher to look through the tiny windows.

Nothing this northern doctor did made any sense. His accent was so thick that he was nearly unintelligible, and if the toy house was some sort of therapeutic device for damaged children then why did the doctor want Christopher to look in it? Shouldn't Daniel be the one to look inside?

But, Christopher did as he was told. He frowned as he looked through the cellophane window. Inside there were three rubber people with painted-on clothes, permanent smiles, and wires beneath their skin. There was nothing charming about these toys. They had no character; they were designed to be universals. They weren't meant to be played with, just to assist in acting out some predetermined interpretation. They weren't toys at all, but tools for reenacting what the doctor called "the family drama." Christopher squinted, and then reached inside the house and dislodged the father doll from his place at the head of a yellow plastic table in the kitchen.

"This is the father?" Chris asked.

The doctor nodded.

During the drive back to Dartmouth, Christopher and Abby quietly quarreled. They made small observations about the road and the weather, but the emotional connection was so fragile that even this much was dangerous.

"The doctor said Daniel would have a better chance if he were to play with it in a therapeutic setting," Christopher said.

Abby had the toy house on her lap. She had all three rubber dolls grasped firmly in her left fist. The mother doll was slightly bent between her index and ring finger.

"That's true," Abby replied.

Christopher said nothing to this. Instead he simply focused on putting his foot down on the gas. Daniel might stack these dolls neatly, or find a way to fit them into cracks or gaps in the woodwork of their home, but Daniel would never play with the toys.

Somebody would have to play with the toys for him and hope that his . . . echolalia, the doctor had called it, would move him to duplicate the act. What dreary games might be brought to life with such toys? Did Abby think that it would be Christopher who would imagine these scenes for their son? Did she expect him to work out what junior would say to the father doll over breakfast?

"Slow down, please," Abby said. She looked like a stranger to Christopher. Where was her easy grace, that smoothness of line he'd seen in her when they were courting? With her stylish hairstyle and perfect clothes, she'd been beautiful, but required protection. Even after this shock she looked pretty, smooth, and presentable, but Christopher knew how thin the surface image was. What seemed durable often turned out to be a brittle façade. Christopher had to handle her with care.

"Did we really need to bring his therapy home? Couldn't we have left the house in the doctor's office? Daniel could play house during his visits, couldn't he?"

Abby turned around and looked at Daniel in the backseat. She reached out to their son and took his hand. Christopher kept his eye on the road and the Channel appeared in front of them as they followed a curve. The Channel was a dark flat green surface spread out into fog.

Chris looked to his left and watched as Abby bent across the passenger seat. With her rear end pointed toward the windscreen she was ridiculous. She was half over the edge, crying into the backseat.

"Daniel?" she asked. "Do you see the mother doll? Do you see how she is sitting next to junior? She is so very fond of her son. Do you see that?"

Christopher felt the pressure in his chest slowly dissolve. He listened to his wife babble at their son, listened to her voice crack, and knew, somehow, that they would be all right. The two of them, mother and child, would survive this. Abby treated Daniel as though he was sick and not the sickness itself. For Abby there was a way forward.

Christopher kept his eyes on the road.

When they arrived in Dartmouth Chris almost flattened a vole right at the start. They stopped at the local hardware store and the rodent scurried through the parking lot, hid itself in the spot where the rear tire met the asphalt. The animal was wedged into the small angle there, and Chris wouldn't have seen the creature at all if Daniel hadn't mentioned it.

"Mouse," Daniel said.

"What's that?"

"Mouse." The boy stopped by the passenger-side door of their blue BMC Morris sedan and pointed at the yellow dividing line. Chris didn't look right away, but placed the planks of timber and cans of orange paint he'd just purchased into the backseat of the sedan first, and only when that business was completed did he turn to look where his son and wife were indicating.

"It might be a mouse," Abby said.

Chris looked and looked but didn't see the brown vole tucked up between the wet leaves on the asphalt and the rubber of his rear tire. Still, it was there. In fact, Chris had difficulty seeing it precisely because it was what his son said it was. He'd become accustomed to Daniel's echolalia, didn't expect the word *mouse* to match up to anything in the real world, and he was looking for something like a coin, something shiny. When Chris finally let himself see the vole, when he recognized the brown furry ball as the mouse in question, he decided that the animal should be made to move.

Chris approached the back tire expecting that the sound of

his feet scraping along the asphalt would set the mouse in motion, but the animal did not budge. Christopher leaned over and tapped the creature with his index finger, thinking the thing was dead and that he'd find it cold to the touch, but while the vole straightened itself out under the tire, it did not otherwise respond to Chris's prodding.

Chris risked a bite and picked the creature up, holding it in the palm of his hand, and the vole set about sniffing and then nipping gently at his fingers. Looking for something to eat, the rodent stuck its head between Chris's pinkie and ring finger and tickled the back of Chris's hand with his whiskers.

"What do you have there?" Abby asked.

"Mouse," Daniel said.

"I believe it's a vole," Chris said. The mouse had a short tail and small ears and Christopher traced the curve of the little creature's face, worked out that it was a field vole and not just a mouse, and then turned his hand to keep the little fur ball from walking off the edge. The vole turned a right angle and stuck his nose up the sleeve of Chris's shirt.

When they got home, above the Harbour Bookshop, Christopher decided to convert the therapeutic dollhouse into an abode for their new rodent friend. He stuffed straw into the tiny master bedroom after removing the king-sized bed with its spongy pink foam mattress and the yellow plastic dresser, and then lined the hallways, kitchen, and living room with the previous day's *Times*.

He handed the furniture and bendable mother, father, and child to Daniel, but Daniel let all of these fall from his hands to the orange carpet. Daniel watched the vole in its empty cardboard box, a box that had once held paperbacks. The vole looked especially small in the left-hand corner.

Christopher cut small squares of green hardware cloth from a bale he'd found in the garden shed and nailed these over the dollhouse windows. Then, when the toy was prepared for it, he opened the front door of the dollhouse for the vole and placed the rodent inside.

"Mouse is home?" Daniel asked.

Chris turned the dollhouse so that Daniel could look inside and watch. The vole was curled up right inside the front door, underneath a plastic chandelier, and leaning against the yellow plastic door. Christopher waited to see if it would move, maybe find its nest, but as always the little guy was perfectly still.

"Out?" Daniel asked.

"You want to take him out again? We just put him in there." But Christopher unlatched the dollhouse and opened it slowly, splayed the two sides of the structure apart, opening it like a book. The vole rolled onto the orange carpet and Christopher picked him up again and held him out to Daniel, but the boy seemed to be focusing first on the orange carpet and then on a standing lamp by the bedroom window. Daniel tracked the curve of the electric cord all the way to the outlet.

After dinner, well after when they could usually expect Daniel to be asleep, Christopher and Abby were interrupted. Daniel opened their bedroom door without knocking and stepped quietly up to the side of their bed, and Christopher didn't notice he was there until he dropped the small animal on his father's head. The thing rolled onto the covers and Chris looked over and met his son's look with his own.

"Daniel? What are you doing?"

"Mouse is dead?" Daniel asked in turn.

Christopher rolled off his wife and sat up under the covers to look closely at the animal his son had dropped. It was broken open, but rather than organs or intestine, cotton was spilling out from the rupture. Turning on the table lamp and holding the dead vole up to the light Chris saw that the rodent had turned pink. Instead of a wet nose and real whiskers it had a sewn-on smile and beads for eyes.

"Oh, Christ!" Abby said.

"An egg?" Daniel asked. This was his television talk. "Every day of your pretty life," he said.

Christopher managed to stay calm. He dressed in his pajamas and went to fetch his box and the three of them looked inside. Chris let Daniel take each item out and hold each up to the light but stopped him from opening the jar of mud. After a while Christopher convinced Daniel to go back to bed.

What had happened was that Daniel had tried to open the house to get the vole, but when the vole had started to run he'd slammed the house closed again at just the wrong moment, splitting the creature open. In Daniel's room there was a spot of blood on the orange carpet and Abby fetched a pail of soapy water and brush while Christopher removed the newspapers, straw, and vole droppings from the dollhouse.

"He killed it?" Abby said.

"It could have happened to any boy," Christopher said.

But, of course, what they had seen when Daniel came into their bedroom couldn't have happened. Not to Daniel or anyone.

Instead of a dead vole they had a broken piglet doll. It didn't make any real sense, but Christopher just shrugged and smiled while Abby hyperventilated.

"Am I going crazy?" she asked.

"Couldn't be both of us at the same time, could it?"

If one of them was anxious the other should see the best of the situation. That had been the arrangement all along, and given that Christopher had switched over into anxiety at the doctor's office while Abby had dedicated herself to carrying on, now that Daniel's vole was a piglet doll it seemed only fair to switch. Abby was allowed to be horrified. They worked it that they might switch off. After all, both horror and optimism seemed to be required.

After cleaning up the mysterious blood spot and seeing Daniel back to his bed, they returned to their bedroom and confirmed their willingness to cooperate, to match each other. This time they weren't interrupted.

PART TWO

1967–MAY 27, 1968

In which Gerrard goes to University, most of France goes on strike, and Christopher Robin finds the North Pole

7

By the time Gerrard was seventeen his dreams were predictable. He hadn't forgotten the police museum, but he figured he was free of it and on his way to reality when the girl in his dorm room took his hand off her shoulder and put it on her breast.

Her name was Natalie and she was working to realize free love. She kissed him but then broke off their embrace in order to read aloud from a copy of Fançoise Sagan's *Bonjour Tristesse*.

"'As his lips touched mine we both began to tremble with pleasure; our kiss was untinged by shame or regret; it was merely a deep searching, interrupted every now and then by whispers.'" She scratched her head. "I don't know. Did you feel any regrets?" she asked.

"Me?"

Gerrard entered Nanterre University in September of 1967 and met Natalie there. He fell in with her crowd, a group of malcontents called Les Détournés. This student group was affiliated with the notorious Situationist International and they said they aimed to disrupt student life in order to change it. The leadership of the SI had given every member of Les Détournés an assignment to this end. Natalie's task was to live out Françoise Sagan's best seller, to make her own life on campus over as a roman à clef. Nobody thought the book had intrinsic merit as literature but it contained utopian, if reified, impulses. Sagan's debauched and bored middle-class family and their sexual misadventures weren't much to contemplate or read about, but the book, when approached as a set of instructions, might be useful. Natalie aimed to discover free love. She wanted to realize it, not only for herself, but for and against the university.

The rules of the university were why they were in Gerrard's dormitory, even though Gerrard had a roommate and they might be interrupted at any moment. Boys were forbidden from visiting the girls' dormitories, and other activities were forbidden as well.

Gerrard put his hand between her legs, felt the coarse wool of her skirt, and she broke away from his embrace again.

"We can't go all the way," she said.

Life at Nanterre University was a kind of purgatory. In 1962 a minister of the army, a man named Mesmer, offered up an air force depot for the site. Paris X Nanterre was conceived as a means of integration, or at least as a repository, for the working-class youth growing up outside of Paris and in its poorer neighborhoods. There were too many children and limited space for them.

The modern working classes needed higher education. They needed training in both the hard and soft sciences as they prepared to enter the workforce, and if there were no jobs for them, the university would be a kind of holding pen. As students they did not count as unemployed.

Gerrard had first noticed Natalie in Neil Lemay's course on social space and Karl Marx. The professor had been lecturing about love from his own book, *The Critique of Everyday Life*.

"In antiquity, passionate love was known, but not individual love, love for an individual. The poets of antiquity wrote of a kind of cosmic, physical, physiological passion, but love for an individual only appears in the Middle Ages within a mixture of Christian and Islamic traditions," Lemay explained. He resembled a French version of Einstein. If Einstein slicked back his wild grey hair he might look a bit like Lemay. The professor paced back and forth in front of a long desk on the platform as he refused to either sit behind one of the microphones like a television personality, or to take up the usual position at the lectern on the right.

"Physical space is modified by representational space. The ultimate victory of representational space is this modification of physical space and all the other manifestations of the representational space. Representations of planning, in diagrams, in lectures, are nothing more than preparations for the modification of physical space. Once physical space is altered, once the real world is occupied by representational space, reclamation of any space for other than ideological use is constrained," Lemay said.

Gerrard imagined representational space as flat and blank, like space between characters in a comic strip panel or between actors on a television screen. Lemay was suggesting that Paris, that modern society, was already contained in exactly this sort of space.

"The extent to which the individual's imagination is kept at bay, kept out of social space, is the extent to which the individual is controlled. It's axiomatic."

The first thing Gerrard noticed about Natalie was how her

blond hair was short like boys' hair, like Twiggy's hair or Juliette Greco's, without being stylish. She had short hair, didn't appear to be wearing makeup, and when she raised her hand to be called on she didn't wait but stood up and started talking.

"What about you, sir? The space of this lecture hall is occupied by the ideology of mass communications and capital. The desk behind you, for instance, conveys authority and is wired with microphones to amplify it. The setup is like something from a television news program," Natalie said. She paused and Lemay leaned on his desk, waiting. Then he turned and spoke into one of the microphones.

"Do you have a question?" he asked.

"I do, sir. What about time? You say that we live in ideological spaces, but it takes time to experience such places."

Gerrard watched Natalie as she listened to Lemay's answer. She met his gaze and seemed to judge his every word. She crossed and uncrossed her arms and leaned forward toward the professor and Gerrard decided he wanted her to notice him, and so while Lemay gave his answer Gerrard formulated another question.

"Would socialist space be rational?"

"What's that?"

"You say socialist space would be directed by the imagination, and well . . . I don't know about you, but my imagination is not always rational. You talked about dreams, and we all know how disordered dreams can be. So, I'm asking, well, is socialism, or is socialist space rational? Is it ordered? And if not, I guess, why not? Can we live with it if it's not, or is it better that it is not?"

"This is a semantic game you're playing," Lemay said.

"What's that?"

"You think the imagination is irrational? That men can't be free and stay sane?"

"I wonder, sir," Gerrard said, "if it's possible. Wouldn't a socialist space be an imaginary space, since it sprang from the imagination? Would it be a dream space?"

"What's irrational is not the imagination, but rather the false consciousness that is produced every day in these representational spaces," Lemay said. "An imaginative socialist would, by definition, be working and living in real or physical space. It has nothing to do with dreams." He stubbed out his cigarette on the desk and then noticed the mark he was making there and tried to brush away the ashes he'd burned into the finish, but to no effect. He looked up, saw Natalie with her hand raised, and called on her without thinking. "Yes, yes?" he said.

"Sir, I wonder if—"

"Wait, you've already asked a question. You don't get to go again. Let somebody else ask."

"You called on me."

"I made a mistake."

"Sir, why should we listen to you about socialism or anything else when you aren't advocating for a revolution?"

Neil Lemay sighed and leaned across his desk, propping himself up with both hands and letting his head hang down. He feigned exhaustion, and then looked fiercely out at her. "Ms. Petrin?"

"Yes."

"I'd appreciate it if you would keep these internal squabbles out of my classroom. You can take your question back to Debord and his café, back to his drunken situation, where it came from, but I won't hear any more of this here."

"In this space your authority can't be questioned?" Natalie asked.

"I wrote about situations and the spectacle a decade before Debord—"

"Thank you, Professor," Natalie cut him short.

At first the professor was a bit stunned and didn't seem to recognize that she'd overtly silenced him, but started shuffling papers on his desk as if he'd lost his place in his lecture. Then he looked at her again and his face turned red. He ran his right hand through his mane of grey hair and let out another sigh. "Okay. Yes. Thank you," he said. "You may go."

The students in the lecture hall didn't move at first, but waited for something more to happen.

"Class dismissed!" Lemay shouted.

Gerrard made sure to catch up with Natalie in the courtyard outside the Science and Humanities building. The building was a concrete block with round windows and a façade that was elevated on round pillars. It was a building that, once he got her talking, Natalie described as having space-age pretensions. Surrounded by glass and concrete, they shared a cigarette and talked.

Natalie was a good talker. She was exactly the opposite of almost everyone Gerrard knew: his peers, his teachers, his mother. None of them believed they could really comprehend the world in its totality. Instead they all chose a part, a skill, a trade, or a thought that applied only to fragments. They did not seek anything whole, but embraced the absurdity of the world with determination. Natalie, on the other hand, explained that she was on the verge of something. She was certain that if she made the effort, if she followed the plot of *Bonjour Tristesse,* she could figure out free love and a lot else.

Gerrard invited Natalie to his dorm room, and when they were behind closed doors, Natalie let him touch her breasts, but she protested when he wanted to go further.

"If we're found out like this it'll be the wrong kind of scandal," she said. "I don't want a bad reputation. Not yet."

"I thought we had to transcend private consciousness."

Natalie kissed him again, but took his hand out of her lap. She let out a long breath and then stood and brushed herself off. "We can only escape the system through private acts," she said. She leaned over, fiercely kissed him again, and then broke it off. "Private acts of refusal," she said.

Nanterre was an American-style university outside of Paris in a suburb that was really a slum. Sunlight and rectangular green lawns defined the space between the cement walkways and the freestanding concrete and Plexiglas awnings at the university. The students were out walking, some of them with bare feet. They squinted in the light, seemingly determined to enjoy the moment, while Gerrard thought up excuses to go indoors. He was one step behind Natalie, watching the way her shoulders moved, the lines of her back under her grey turtleneck shirt.

"I think this place, the educational track that we're on, it's a dead end. If things went on like this, the best I can hope for is to end up as a housewife for some boy I meet in Paris. I might pick up a husband from the Sorbonne. That's the best future for me, the worst is that I end up like you. We'll join each other on the unemployment line here in Nanterre," Natalie said.

"I can see that," Gerrard said.

"The solution is to say goodbye to this happy nothing called modern education and say *bonjour, tristesse* instead," Natalie said.

Gerrard took her hand and diverted her from the sidewalk. They tramped across the wet grass leaving tracks in the sod, and then stopped underneath an imported elm. Gerrard sat in the wet grass and then patted his lap indicating that Natalie should sit. He put his arm around Natalie's waist and then leaned forward and whispered in her ear.

"Where? You have some plan for where we should go to do this. Somewhere private?" she asked.

Gerrard blushed, but then he ran his hands along her ribcage, feeling the nubs of her cotton turtleneck. He thought of the way it felt to touch her skin.

"You were going to tell me about a different book. About a bear?" she asked.

"Yes. A British bear. A stuffed British bear named Pooh."

"I've heard of him. But I thought this Pooh was American. A Disney character like Mickey Mouse.

"No. He is a bear of letters. This bear is the product of the mind of the author A. A. Milne. Pooh is a character invented in order to entertain Milne's young son Christopher Robin."

"Ah. And why do you want to tell me about Pooh? Do you think I'm a child?"

"No, not at all. In fact I think you are grown-up enough to hear about how Pooh found the North Pole."

In the Pooh story Christopher Robin and Pooh set off to find the North Pole, even though they didn't know precisely what it was. They brought along all of their friends: the donkey, the pig, the rabbit, and all of his relations. Along the way they ate all of their provisions: the thistles brought along for the donkey and an entire jar of honey. It was rough going, and then it turned for the worse when a baby kangaroo fell into the river.

It was then, when things were getting worse, that Pooh found the North Pole. He rescued the kangaroo with it.

"How did he find it?" Natalie asked.

"He didn't even know he'd found it at first. He just needed a stick and it was only after the fact, after Pooh rescued the kangaroo, that Christopher Robin decided that the stick was it. Christopher announced that they'd found the North Pole."

Gerrard hugged Natalie tighter to him, squeezing her around her waist. "We might not always know when we've turned a corner or broken free until after it happens."

Natalie turned to face him, gave him a quick kiss on the lips, and then started to stand up. She glanced toward the Plexiglas awnings and concrete walkways, back toward the patterned life of Nanterre, and laughed.

"Do you want to find the North Pole?" she asked.

"But of course," Gerrard said.

8

Christopher and his family approached Cotchford Farm on foot, walking from where he'd parked their car. From the front gate his father's mansion looked something like a jigsaw puzzle that hadn't been put together properly. The front gable abruptly stopped where the architect had drawn a vertical line; this gave the estate a fractured quality. This disjointed appearance along with the tall chimneys, Christopher's own nostalgia, and the smell of sod all combined to make the place seem fictional. They were headed into a house built under the name of Sanders, into Pooh's corner, and as they approached Daniel started babbling.

"Never," Daniel said. "Never. Never go without a Capstan."

It was an advertising jingle for a cigarette. "What's the matter, Daniel?" Christopher asked.

"Never," Daniel said.

"Come on now."

"I don't want to see Grandpa," Daniel said. He could find his own words.

"Oh. You won't have to. You won't see Grandpa. It's your grandmother who is waiting. Grandfather is gone now."

"Never," Daniel said. But, he started walking again.

His father had been sick for a while, been very near the end a number of times, and now that it had finally happened Christopher wished that it could have come sooner. His father might've died in London last year. It would have suited him better. He could've died as a satirist and intellectual rather than as a children's author, and in London Christopher could have escaped the memories just by walking.

Stepping inside the foyer his mother told them she was glad to see him, to see all of them. She still wore her hair short, like a flapper girl, but her dress was orange polyester. She showed them to the guest room and Christopher almost expected that he'd find his teddy bear waiting for him on the quilted bedclothes, but of course the toys were on display in the office of Father's publisher in America.

Returning to Cotchford Farm, Chris found the place very much as it had been and yet, at the same time, entirely different. A smell of medicine clung to the air, an antiseptic sting, and there was something fragile seeming about the old estate.

"It's nearly teatime," Abby said. She was only observing the fact of it and not commenting on any thirst or hunger.

How was it that Christopher's strongest memories of his father weren't of him, but of his absence? Surely there were many times when they'd worked together on some project or other. There had been many instances when he'd been solidly present. Christopher could remember how his father had taught him the basics of cricket—how to bend one's knees and extend the arm while bowling, how to swing the bat, and when Chris had found the bat to be unwieldy, when he'd been clumsy, his father had patted him on the head and told him that soon enough the game would find him.

But, what Christoper remembered most clearly was seeing his father from afar.

Christopher had been introduced to a journalist from London. She'd been quite impressed with the farm, had commented on the roof beams; she'd said the beams looked as though they might once have been ship's timbers, and then she'd settled in on the yellow-and-gold sofa. Then his father had called Christopher over and introduced him to her as "our boy."

"How do you do?" Christopher said.

He drifted out of the room while the reporter went on being impressed. Christopher changed into his Wellingtons and wandered out the back door to the duck pond. He and the cat, a black cat named Bianca, sat together on the edge of the pond and watched mallards dunk their heads and catch minnows in their beaks while in the house father held forth on the subject of Christopher's toy bear. Father always complained about being asked always and only about the bear. He had written better books, new books, so why didn't the pretty journalist from London ask about those books instead?

Christopher must've found a copy of the interview later on. Perhaps he'd read it in the *Times* that very week, or maybe it had been years later when he'd come across the clipping in a drawer, but however he found it she'd asked his father whether being a household name might be a burden for Christopher Robin, and his father had not been sure how to answer.

Finally he said that the question had truly never occurred to him before, but that everyone had to live up to something or down to something.

Sometime after the interview Christopher tried to lose the toys. He wandered across the bridge in Ashdown, stopped at the wood rail and looked down into the slowly moving water below, and then decided to leave the stuffed donkey behind. He propped the toy up so that the toy was sitting on his hind legs and the little animal's head dangled down and rested on the wooden slats at the edge.

Christopher left Piglet in a clump of thistle, placed Kanga by a desiccated tree stump, put Rabbit in a hole he'd dug up near the perimeter of Cotchford Farm, and placed the bear in a potted plant on the stone walk near the servant entrance. The bear looked back in the direction of his fallen friends. Pooh was concerned for them.

Christopher went inside and let Nanny draw him a bath. He enjoyed the warm water, washed his hair and dunked his head, got back out of the tub and made sure to thoroughly dry himself. Nanny helped him. She tousled his hair. She rubbed and rubbed his damp head, until he stopped dripping. And it was only then, when he was changing into his nightclothes, that Christopher pretended to remember.

"Where is my bear?" he asked.

"Your what, Billy?"

After Father's storybooks had been so successful the toys that had inspired them had become his father's toys even if they were still kept in the nursery.

"What were you thinking? Where was your head?" Nanny asked.

They found the animals in the mud, on a stump, and still waiting on Poohsticks Bridge, and when they returned to the house Nanny quietly hand washed the toys in the same tub Christopher had bathed in.

Instead of stuffed toys Christopher and his family found a New-
ton's cradle on the desk in the guest room. There were five metal
balls suspended by strings, and Daniel lifted the ball to his right
and let go, setting the balls to clacking.

"It's teatime," Abby said.

It was teatime, she was right, and they ought to pop down to
the kitchen to see if they were expected there.

"Daphne and Alan often had tea in the nook off the kitchen,"
Christopher said. Christopher called his parents by their first
names when he spoke to his wife, as he felt it was less confusing
to refer to them this way, and if they were going to name everyone by their familial titles then she would have to refer to her
father, for instance, as both her father and Christopher's uncle
Lawrence, and she would refer to her mother as Aunt Judy? All
of it seemed unnecessary. Her father was Lawrence, and Christopher's father was Alan. That was simple, and if it was also a bit
modern, well the impropriety didn't bother him.

When they arrived downstairs they found that Daphne wasn't
there, although she'd left a plate of mallows on the table in the
nook. Christopher's mother had been waylaid from tea by a visi-
tor. She was showing this young man around the backyard.
There was Christopher's mother with her grey hair and stooped
dignity, walking through the garden with a man with long blond
hair. The young man was wearing blue jeans, motorcycle boots,
and a shirt patterned after the American flag.

"What's this?" Christopher asked.

"Slow down, dear," Abby said. Christopher turned to his
wife but she was talking to Daniel who'd started in on the mal-

lows. He had two of them in his mouth and another was melting in his hand.

"I'll be just a moment."

It turned out that the gentleman in the American flag was a British pop star. The man's name, Brian Jones, meant nothing to Christopher but he did recognize the name of the band. He'd heard of the musical group called the Rolling Stones. Brian Jones was in the process of purchasing Cotchford Farm, and Christopher's mother was obliged to accompany the young man as he surveyed the property.

"Are you Christopher Robin then?" Brian Jones asked.

"Christopher Milne, actually. How do you do?"

"Very sorry to hear about your father. I quite liked him. He was a funny chap, wasn't he?"

"That was his living."

"Well, my condolences and I'm sorry to interrupt. It's just this was scheduled ahead."

Christopher scratched his head.

"We are selling Cotchford Farm to Mr. Jones," his mother informed him.

"I would've postponed except for I'm going on tour. It had to be today." The pop star in their garden leaned against the stone statue by the walkway. He put his left elbow on the stone head of a boy named Christopher Robin and the statue seemed to shift a bit.

"Please. You're going to topple that."

"It's you, isn't it?"

"Don't do that."

"Don't worry. It's solid."

Brian Jones put his foot against the pedestal that the statue of

Christopher Robin was set on and he pushed off it, jumping back. "I'd need a crane to topple that monster," Brian Jones said. "That fellow isn't going anywhere."

Christopher realized the pop star was quite right. Even now, after his father the writer was dead, the little boy made of stone continued on. Christopher might never get away from himself.

Christopher stepped slowly down the hall in his socked feet, especially careful to step softly as he made his way past the master bedroom where his mother slept, and slowing still more as he passed the small bedroom and office where his father had spent so many years in a kind of solitary confinement with only his typewriter and books to keep him company. Chris glanced down at the intricate pattern in the oriental rug, at the crazy red, blue, and beige mandala under his feet.

Christopher could not sleep at Cotchford Farm, but was drawn into the halls, compelled to pace. It was late, sometime in the very early morning, perhaps past two, and Christopher switched on the Adams style bronze chandelier in the drawing room. He approached the piano on the north wall and touched the sheet music propped up on the stand. The music for Bill Murray's "Shine On Harvest Moon" had yellowed.

Christopher decided to make himself a cup of tea.

The kitchen was tidy and modern, and Christopher wondered when his mother had purchased the electric stove. He boiled water in an orange enamel teakettle and searched for a teapot but found the good china had already been packed away. There were only a few coffee mugs in the cabinet, coffee mugs his father had received as a gift from Disney. Christopher chose the cup featuring a cartoon deer. He only steeped his tea for ten seconds or so as he'd picked a black tea and he still had ambitions toward sleep.

Back in the drawing room Christopher sat on the knit coverlet that covered the cushioned seat of the Queen Anne wingback chair. The vase of flowers on the small wood table in the centre of the room contained an amazing display of orange lilies in full bloom, but the seams on each plastic bud were visible even in the dim light from the chandelier. Christopher took a sip of his weak tea and realized that his father was really and truly dead. Cotchford Farm was a memorial now, but then it always had been.

The writer Father had admired most was Thackeray. Father had followed Thackeray's example and written for *Punch*, and Father had built his vacation home in Thackeray's honor, but now Thackeray was remembered mostly as a satirist who wrote against the times and values that he, in fact, cherished most. Thackeray and Father would be misremembered. Thackeray would be misremembered through *Vanity Fair*, and Father would be misremembered through that stupid bear. Buying Cotchford Farm had been an act of faith on Father's part, and over the years the estate had been transformed into a religious institution of some sort. Kings and queens didn't matter anymore and everyone was now a humanist, but a man of letters needed the right furniture and the correct table. These decisions still had relevance and importance.

Thackeray had developed a knack for describing the furniture of the seventeenth century precisely because these sorts of objects were all that remained of the old aristocracy, but now Father's silver vase contained flowers from Disney's America. Cotchford Farm had been invaded by the new vision, and Christopher was sure that the pop star who was purchasing the estate could be relied upon to destroy whatever vestiges of the old monarchist ways remained.

Christopher's tea was barely stronger than water. Sitting up at that time of night he decided he needed something more substantial to reassure him, but something that would work in the opposite direction. He wanted whiskey, but he wasn't entirely sure where to find such stuff. A good amount of the estate had already been packed into crates and boxes, and his parents hadn't entertained during the past few years in any case. It was quite possible that there was none of it, and Christopher did not want to set off on a fool's errand. Still, if there was no whiskey, or none in evidence, then Christopher would seek out the words of Thackeray instead. Thackeray had always steadied his father; perhaps they would soothe him as well. Christopher would seek out *The History of Henry Esmond*.

Groping in the cramped darkness of his father's bedroom, Christopher grasped air before finding the switch for the overhead light. Then, with the yellow light switched on, Christopher was surprised not so much by the sight of the empty mahogany shelves, the clean and polished surface of his father's little desk, or the absence of his father's chair, but by the absence of boxes. There were no books, no papers and pens. His father's closet was empty as well. There was nothing in it but the wood rail along the top. There were not even wire coat hangers left behind.

Finally he found it. There was a cardboard box folded shut and pushed half under Father's stripped bed. Christopher got down on hands and knees to search through it and discovered bed linen.

Where were his father's books and papers? What had his mother done with his father's effects? Father had kept on writing even after his heart surgery in 1966, which had been a procedure that had seemed to affect his mind as much as his heart. Christopher had been surprised by how little of his father had remained after the surgery. He'd still managed to appear neat and tidy, and he'd clung to his dignity, but at a high cost. Christopher visited in the summer of '66, visited them in London, and Father had sat at the dining-room table for tea in his dinner jacket. His posture was perfect, but as Christopher watched his father eat his pudding with raisins he could see how much effort was required to maintain the ritual. Still, Father's spoon did not shake in his hand. He did not spill any of the pudding on his lap, and in this way the tea was a success. Even after he had become childlike and slow in his daily life, even after simple interactions with people proved to be beyond his capacity, Father had continued writing. He'd gone on producing three to four pages a day just as he had for decades.

There was not a trace of these writings.

Back in the drawing room Christopher stood next to the table with the plastic flowers and found a small pile of mail next to the vase. Putting down the coffee mug directly on the wood, he riffled through the envelopes until he came upon a letter addressed to his father. Opening it he discovered a check from America, a check for a quite goodly amount. Christopher felt slightly sick looking at the number, and eventually placed the check back in its envelope. He placed the envelope back on the table between the Disney mug and a copy of the most current edition of *Punch* magazine.

Instead of Punch the puppet there was a naked lady on the cover of the magazine. Apparently attempting to satirize *Playboy,* to satirize what could not be satirized, the headline across the top of the magazine promised the sight of a nude Hugh

Hefner inside. Hugh Hefner was *Punch*'s featured Playmate of the Month.

Punch was parodying pornography, while his mother and soon enough Christopher himself would be living off of American cartoons.

Sitting in the early morning's electric light, drinking cold and watery tea, and looking for a peek of a nipple on the cover of *Punch,* Christopher almost felt guilty. His father might be dead, but he was still hovering nearby, and Christopher knew that his father was disappointed by the whole dreadful picture.

9

Natalie said she didn't know how Gerrard fit into her project with Sagan's novel and so he tried giving her an alternate novel. He came to her in late October with a dream he'd had that, upon awakening, he'd decided was based on Orwell's *1984*.

"How about George Orwell instead?" Gerrard asked.

In Gerrard's dream the two of them agreed to finally have sex, but they had to leave the university to do it. They took the train into Paris, to a platform in the Gare du Nord, and held each other. She put her hands under his cotton shirt, and he touched her neck, but they stopped with that. They were caught out on the platform. Dr. Neil Lemay spotted them there, mocked them for their timidity. He told them that he could help them find a private room. He scratched at his beard, looked the two of them over, up and down.

Lemay took them to a bookstore, it turned out it was his store, and Gerrard bought a journal with cream-colored blank pages.

"There was a room above the shop, and Lemay was willing to

rent it out by the hour. We went up rickety stairs and found the bed mattress was barely acceptable. We worried about bugs," Gerrard said.

In his dream Gerrard spotted a portly working-class woman out the window. She was hanging laundry in the next yard.

"The woman is beautiful," Natalie had said. "Turn around." When Gerrard turned back she'd removed her skirt and sweater, and her cheeks and lips were a brighter shade of pink than they'd been a moment earlier.

"Lipstick and blush," Natalie interjected. "Like Julia."

"I hadn't noticed that you'd been without makeup, but when you put on that little color I could tell the difference." In the dream she'd kissed him and Gerrard had caught sight of his reflection in the window. Instead of the portly laundress he saw his own face. His lips had been pink with lipstick.

Natalie kissed him there, in reality, on the concrete bench, and suggested that they should skip out on the professor and his class, that they didn't need him for what they wanted.

"I think Lemay is confusing you. France is, for the moment anyhow, a capitalist country. We don't have to find some secret hovel to have sex in. Orwell wasn't talking about France."

Gerrard objected to her logic. "The dorms are off-limits, the bushes aren't tall enough to hide anything. You make it sound simple."

"It is simple. All we need is to find the commodity for sex. It's the same for everything, right? In this case what we need is an automobile."

Natalie's neighbor in the girls' dormitory had a Citroën 2CV, a convertible with red leather seats and seat belts, and Natalie managed to convince the girl to lend it to her.

Gerrard was behind the wheel as they headed west, to the

countryside. He tested out how the automobile handled. Natalie wore a straw sunhat despite the February weather, and they left the top down for the first few miles until what had been a light sprinkle turned into a steady rain.

Gerrard let his eyes drift off the road for a moment. She had her feet out the window and the muscles in her thighs were visible.

He was a little lost, just east of Saint-Germain-en-Laye, and on a dirt road that seemed to stretch on indefinitely. Gerrard turned back to driving, and he watched the windshield wipers keeping time. It was green outside the automobile, green and wet. They were rolling through a forest on mud tracks in the grass. Natalie took off her sandals and again stuck her feet, now bare, out the passenger window. Washing her feet in the rain she leaned against Gerrard and sighed.

"Tell me about your first time," she said.

"What?"

"This isn't it, is it? I don't think I could handle being the first."

Gerrard told her not to worry.

"But, you aren't going to tell me."

"What about you?"

"You want to know about my first?" she asked. "I'll tell."

"No. Well . . . I don't know."

Natalie tipped her sunhat forward so that the brim covered her eyes. She told him that her first boyfriend was a boy on the track team in high school, that his name was Patrick, and that he was very attentive.

"Is that what you want? Attention?" he asked.

She sat up straight, put her feet back in the vehicle, and looked out the windshield. She let the wipers move ten or twenty times before answering.

"I'm confused about what I want. It seems like romance is a

trap. We invest everything, look for all of life in these boy and girl antics, but how can romance or love change the university, the factory, or any of it," she said.

"'The student, if she rebels at all, must first rebel against her studies. But, at the same time, since she is a product of modern society just like Godard or Coca-Cola, her extreme alienation can only be fought through the struggle against the whole society,'" Gerrard recited slowly, drawing each word from his memory and considering it before saying it aloud.

"That's from the Strasbourg pamphlet," Natalie said. The pamphlet had come out of the University of Strasbourg two years earlier and it had been a scandal. The students responsible had been expelled for publishing the tract with union funds. The pamphlet was considered a big success by Les Détournés because everyone, especially teenagers, had read about the prank in the newspapers. Many had read the pamphlet itself.

"Do you remember what they said about sex?" Natalie asked.

He didn't remember, or only vaguely.

"'Thirty years after Wilhelm Reich's excellent lessons the student still clings to the most traditional forms of erotic behavior, reproducing at this level the general relations of class society,'" Natalie said.

Natalie and Gerrard parked in the forest of Saint-Germain-en-Laye, along a meander of the Seine. Gerrard stopped the car among the trees and worried about how he was going to find his way back to the main road. He wondered if he'd have to go in reverse the entire way.

"Nice," Natalie said. "This is like a holiday at the end of the world." She kissed him and then pulled away again. He watched her pupils move back and forth as she scanned his face.

She adjusted the front seat so that it tipped all the way back, but getting out of their clothes was not as easy as might have been hoped for. Natalie had to lift herself up off him and press her bare ass up against the window as Gerrard struggled to get his trousers down. She left her shirt on, but unbuttoned the front, and then stopped Gerrard from trying to pull his T-shirt off over his head.

"It's okay. We're naked enough. Let's just put it in now," she said.

They had sex in the front seat, slowly and awkwardly. And as Gerrard neared climax, as he found a rhythm and a way to ignore the way his skin was sticking to the upholstery, as he focused on how Natalie felt against him, about the way she smelled and breathed as she moved, Gerrard wondered how he'd ended up fucking in a convertible.

After working this way and that trying out rhythms, Natalie's movements became frantic. She seemed to reach climax quickly, and when she came she shouted, "Hello, sadness!"

10

They had breakfast on campus, looking out the pane glass windows to watch other students cross the green lawn.

The café was noisy with talk and music from a Jupiter Jukebox. Johnny Hallyday was singing "San Francisco" as Natalie and Gerrard found a table. They didn't talk to each other, not right away, but took sips from cups of onion soup and coffee.

Natalie lit a Gitanes cigarette as she silently reread Sagan's book, while Gerrard stirred his soup and sulked. How was it that so little had changed between them?

"My problem is that I like Bergson," Natalie said.

"What's that?"

"The girl protagonist Cecile, she goes on and on about how she's can't stand philosophy, how she can't understand Bergson," Natalie explained. "But I quite liked Bergson."

Gerrard swirled small packets of sugar into the bitter cups of coffee they'd purchased.

"It's still bitter," he said. Gerrard poured more sugar into his coffee and then stared into the small cup as the sugar dissolved.

He watched bubbles on the surface swirl and break apart as the sugar and coffee mixed.

Gerrard took another sip of onion soup as Natalie continued reading. Sometimes her lips moved as she repeated the same lines over and over again to herself in an attempt to do something new with them.

"Listen," she said. "'I thought of Cyril. I would have liked to be caressed, consoled, reconciled with myself.'"

"What of it?"

"Do you feel reconciled with yourself?" she asked.

"The problem is that you're trying to live out that novel as if you're not fictional already," Gerrard said. "Haven't you noticed? Our names are already like the characters in your novel: Gerrard and Natalie?"

"Oh, yes," Natalie said. "I see what you mean. We're both of us characters in a novel."

"Either we're in a novel, or a dream, or some other unreal thing. There's something unfinished about us."

Natalie covered her face with her hand, shielded her eyes from the sight of him. Then she took Gerrard's hand and kissed his fingers. "I know the people who wrote the Strasbourg essay. Do you want to meet them?" she asked.

Gerrard said he did. Of course he did.

Natalie leaned in close, so that her lips brushed against his ear, and then whispered a line from her book: "'I wanted to bruise him, so that he would not be able to forget me for a single moment all the evening, and would dream of me all night long.'"

She sat back again and took a sip from one of her paper cups. "Terrible," she said, but it wasn't clear if she was referring to the novel or the soup.

"I'm not joking, though," Gerrard said. "We're living out some sort of fiction."

The sound of Edith Piaf singing "Milord" came from the jukebox as Gerrard tried to explain it to her.

He'd come to regard dreaming as a concept rather than an experience. In lycée he'd read André Breton, Louis Althusser, and other Marxist philosophers who explained that dreaming wasn't just something you did while you were asleep, but it was pervasive in the waking world. For Althusser, for example, the dream reconstituted itself daily in the material world.

You could find the dream in the factories, in the arcades, and on the streets. The dream was what guided you through relationships. The dream told you who you were and what was expected of you.

Gerrard had also read about the Dreamtime and the Aboriginal concept of the dream. For the Nunga people the dream was the moment of creation and it resided outside of historical time. It was a realm, a land, accessible through ritual storytelling.

"Or you can find it in a pop song," Gerrard said.

As he listened he decided Piaf was a contradiction. Her sadness opposed the grandeur and conformity contained in her chosen genre. She was a woman born in a brothel and trained to turn her misery into sound, and "Milord" was both a promise of liberation and a command to conform. She voiced the collective despair of the proletariat but made that despair a romance. She sold the masses back their will to survive as a kind of rebellion.

"Piaf was one of your father's favorites?"

Natalie put down Sagan's book.

"Yes."

He'd listened to Piaf when he was a teenager, during the occupation, and he wouldn't tolerate talk of Edith the collaborator, the drug addict, the tragedy. Piaf represented France before the war. Her songs were unpolluted by the German occupation, and uncorrupted by imported American rhythms.

"Your father took you to the demonstration," Gerrard said. "You saw what happened to the Algerians."

"What?" Natalie wrapped her arms around herself, knocking over a cup of what was originally onion soup but looked more like mud as it spread across the table.

"At the Rex cinema your dad held your hand tight, bruised it because he was terrified of losing you in the crowd."

"How do you know that?" Natalie asked.

Gerrard told her that they were characters, that he could read or dream ahead, and that the song "Milord" was what connected one scene to the next.

When, in 1961, the police opened fire into a crowd of thousands of French Algerians dressed in their Sunday best, Natalie and her father hid under the marquee. There was blood on the street, on the cobblestones, and they were screaming. Everybody was screaming against the bullets, against the death, and in the chaos the police started to work with clubs and handcuffs. As the Algerians retreated, trampling one another to get away, the police rounded up a few survivors and pulled them in.

"We crouched in an alcove of a British import shop, I can remember the boxes of tea, chamomile and orange spice. Our breath made clouds," Natalie said. "My father was swearing under his breath. He had lost his camera in the crowd and kept peeking around the corner, looking toward the muffled screams, glancing down at the sidewalk, staring into the confusion looking for the orange-and-green shoulder strap reflecting light from between scuffling feet. He didn't spot it."

Natalie's father, she told Gerrard, was a liberal journalist. He'd taken her along to the demonstrations because the word was that the event was going to be huge, that it was going to be peaceful. A hundred thousand Algerians were to march through Paris, but the chief of police had blocked off the Metro stations in Arab neighborhoods. Ten thousand police were working at holding it all back. Her father hadn't known that the officials of Paris were willing to kill that day. He hadn't known that people would be fishing the bloated bodies of men, women, and children out of the Seine for days after.

The police pushed them under, drowned them, made them disappear.

"You and your father witnessed a massacre," Gerrard said.

"How did you know?" Natalie asked.

"This coffee is terrible," Gerrard said. "I can't get it sweet enough." He tried a spoonful of Natalie's onion soup, but the soup tasted terrible too. It tasted like mud. Gerrard asked Natalie for one of her cigarettes. Maybe the smoke would get rid of the bad taste.

"We were lucky not to be Algerian or be mistaken for Algerian. The police didn't shoot us. We were grateful for that," she said. "He'd lost his camera."

Her father had been terrified after, kept telling her over and over again that they weren't to speak of what they'd seen. His daughter couldn't be heard talking about that, about the demonstration.

"They drowned children in the Seine," Natalie said. "But wait, how did you know?"

"You want to know how? I told you. We're unfinished, fictional," he said.

Natalie looked out the glass wall of the café at the sunrise. The orange sky hadn't changed since they'd gotten up that morning. She took a sip of her coffee and Gerrard took a sip from his. It was still hot but terribly bitter.

"You have to test reality. That's how you do it. You test the present like you would if you thought you were dreaming. Pinch your nose and hold it. Can you still breathe? Find a light switch and flip it, does the lighting in the room change? Look at the clock. Can you figure out the time?"

Natalie stood up from the table, walked to the front of the café, and looked out at the orange sky. She found the light switch and turned off the overhead light, but nothing happened. She turned and looked back at Gerrard, and then pinched her nose for a moment and waited to gasp.

Something was wrong. Natalie pushed her hair out of her face and then came back to the table and sat down again. She picked up her coffee and hesitantly took a sip. It was bitter.

"I'm asleep," she said. "I'm dreaming."

11

Natalie took him to see Debord not long after that. When she and Gerrard arrived at Chez Isou, Debord's gang was passing a mimeographed copy of the comic strip *Barbarella* around their table. Chez Isou was a tiny café on Rue du Four, a sliver of space in a limestone building where oversized tables were surrounded by assorted wicker and wooden chairs, tiny booths, benches, all of it wedged in by a scratched-up Queen Anne upright piano. It was where the revolutionary members of Parisian bohemian life got drunk on red wine and gin, and Natalie was glad to be there even if she didn't look forward to Debord asking after her progress with the Sagan book. That had been his assignment for her and she was pretty sure he wouldn't approve of how she'd been handling the project.

Someone dropped the comic strip in front of them and Gerrard picked it up and held it so she could see. A male astronaut in an orange space suit and a fishbowl helmet climbed across the bare breast of a statue of Barbarella and in the next panel two female astronauts were shown climbing out her mouth. The girl astronauts wore green space suits with fishbowls and held phallic ray guns. They shot white clouds over the head of the man in the orange suit.

The text in the girl's speech balloon had been altered:

In the spectacle's basic practice of incorporating into itself all the fluid aspects of human activity so as to possess them in a congealed form, and of inverting living values into purely abstract values, we recognize our old enemy the commodity.

Guy had his arm around the neck of another student, some rebel in a leather jacket from the Sorbonne, but Guy was wearing a dingy off-white wool sweater and looked too French, too middle-aged for the scene he was in. Sure, most of the café-scene radicals were old, in their midthirties, some even in their forties, but Guy looked particularly old. He was sitting at the head of the table with his much younger Greek girlfriend Isadora standing behind him, with his arm around the shoulder of this boy from the Sorbonne, and he was clearly already a bit drunk and still drinking steadily.

Isadora was playing with Debord's spectacles. She put them on and then put her hands on Debord's head and played with his hair. Finally she returned his glasses to him and sat down beside him, to his left.

Natalie tried to get his attention. "I've brought a friend with me," she said as she moved around the table.

"This is your Cyril, yes?" Guy asked Natalie. "You've been working on living out the Sagan book?"

Cyril was the name of Cecile's young lover in *Bonjour Tristesse*. She ignored his challenge. "His name is Gerrard," Natalie said. "And he's got a game to teach us."

"A game of strategy?" Guy Debord asked. Madame Isou

came by with a bottle of gin and poured it into metal cups for Isadora and Natalie.

"It's a game about time," Gerrard said. "More of a technique than a game really."

"It's a dreaming game," Natalie said.

Most of the crew was already drunk. They were giggling over their altered comic book, smoking cigarettes and clapping one another on the back, and not listening. Natalie ran her fingers along the tabletop, accidentally fingering cigarette ash, and then playing with the ash on purpose, drawing a face with it. She drew a smile, and then brushed the smile away.

"A game about time and dreams?" Guy asked. "Dreams as such are a dead end. Besides, time has stopped. The present is static. Fashion itself, clothes, music, philosophy, all of it has stopped. The capitalist world wants us to forget the past and give up on the future," he said.

"This game involves remembering," Gerrard said.

But Debord wasn't listening. He wanted to talk about Françoise Sagan and how the author he'd selected for Natalie had been making vaguely leftist statements from her Ferrari as of late. Debord loved reading about the idle rich because these stories illustrated both how hollow the utopias on offer always turned out to be and how the libertine impulse was caught up in another better one. Françoise Sagan and free love were grasping after something else, something like emancipation proper.

Natalie had heard all this before.

"You know how *Bonjour Tristesse* could have been a better book?" she asked.

"How?"

"If Cecile had done her homework and learned something. That way the whole stupid mess would've turned out differently."

Guy leaned across the table and smiled. "Let's have another glass of wine." He poured from his own bottle for Natalie and for himself. It was white wine, a bit too sweet, but she swallowed it, gulped it all down in one go, while Debord took a small sip from his glass.

In Sagan's book the main character had broken up her father's second marriage in order to avoid reading Henri Bergson. Cecile's father's new wife expected that Cecile would pass her philosophy paper and make something of herself, but she'd wanted nothing more than to drift from beach to restaurant, or to spend her time between clean sheets in a hotel bed where she might count the motes in the air. Avoiding the hard work of study had been one of Cecile's conscious motivations in the book, whereas Natalie had read Bergson, Sartre, and many others. What's more Natalie thought that Cecile wouldn't have had to give up much in the service of Bergson's phenomenology. Bergson had, after all, said that sex appeal was the keystone of human civilization.

Gerrard put down his glass. "'In reality, the past is preserved by itself automatically. In its entirety, probably, it follows us at every instant; all that we have felt, thought, and willed from our earliest infancy is there, leaning over the present, which is about to join it, pressing against the portals of consciousness that would fain leave it outside.'" He was quoting Bergson. "That's what my game is about. It involves drawing the past into the present. Using memory as a catalyst to change the present."

Guy wanted another drink and poured again from the bottle the lady had left behind for them. The three of them sat behind glasses of wine and watched the café scene move. Even though they were all sitting still everyone was also moving fast, faster than

Natalie could track. Isadora was a blur to her, mostly yellow and red. The wine bottles were emptying out around them, the conversations a meaningless jumble of words.

"Airplanes, automobiles, street lamps, telephones, umbrellas, some everyday consumer items like detergents and Orangina," Gerrard explained to her.

"What are you saying?"

Gerrard told her about Guy Debord, about how Debord's family had driven to Cannes from Paris, directly south, when the Nazis took Paris. They'd driven to Cannes in Debord's mother's 1929 Traction Avant. It was a fancy car, one of the few luxuries they'd held on to after the Depression hit. By the time of the German invasion the Debords' prospects were nil, but they escaped Paris in time.

Natalie hadn't thought of Debord's childhood before, or of how he might have survived the German occupation.

Isadora and Guy were by the piano now, and Isadora took a gulp from a metal cup, sat down on the piano bench, and started playing France Gall's "Jazz à Gogo."

"I know what we need is jazz with a gogo," she sang.

"Down with yé-yé!" Natalie shouted back at her. "Down with the society of France Gall!"

But Isadora just kept singing the insipid yé-yé song.

Everyone continued drinking, but Guy was the most inebriated by the time Natalie and Gerrard stood to go. He picked up the *Barbarella* comic strip and pressed it against the side of the wineglasses he carried as he followed them to the door.

Outside they stopped and discussed the best way back to Nanterre, neither of them sure when the last train left.

"I want to tell you a story," Guy said. "Do you have time for one more drink?" He had three glasses with him, and they each took a glass and toasted each other. Guy Debord took a small cautious sip from his own.

"I've lost a few to madness," Guy said.

"Lost what?" Gerrard asked.

"Friends. I've lost them to madness, Gerrard."

He told them of a Russian comrade who had contributed great things to the revolution back in 1953. Back then they'd still considered themselves artists, and his friend had thought himself a poet. They'd worked together, this poet and Debord, on theories of urbanism. They'd worked to understand social space.

"His ideas about architecture, about articulating time and space, were quite good. He could write." Debord leaned against the wrought iron fence that bordered Chez Isou's outside tables. He looked up at an electric street lamp on Rue du Four and remembered. "'We are bored in the city, there is no longer any Temple of the Sun. Between the legs of the women walking by, the Dadaists imagined a monkey wrench and the surrealists a crystal cup.' Ivan Chtcheglov was quite good, but he went mad. They locked him away, and ultimately they destroyed him. The psychiatric doctors wiped him clean with drugs and electricity."

"What kind of madness was it?" Natalie asked.

"The usual kind. He believed we were secretly directed by the Dalai Lama. He thought that there was a black light in the Eiffel Tower," Guy said.

"A black light?"

"He resolved to destroy the tower. Went out one night to topple the thing but ended up somewhere like this. He ended up drinking, and then destroying the wineglasses, the dishes. Then he started throwing tables and chairs," Guy said.

The three of them stood under light from street lamps. Guy blew out puffs of smoke from his cigar and took sips from his wineglass.

"We should be going. The Metro," Natalie said.

"His wife turned him in to the police. He was declared insane and then they destroyed his mind," Guy said. "You should put this dream game aside. It leads nowhere but to mysticism at best and psychosis at worst."

"You think so?" Gerrard asked.

"I know what game you should play instead."

Gerrard borrowed a Gitanes cigarette from Natalie and then took a swig of wine because he didn't like the taste.

"Work on derailing things," Debord said. He showed Gerrard the comic strip page from *Barbarella,* held it up for him to read under the street lamp.

"We've seen it," Natalie said.

"Any elements, no matter where they are taken from, can be used to make new combinations. We might derail whole cities?"

"I don't know," Gerrard said.

"Forget what I said before. Life is disorienting. That's just how it is. Madness is the risk we take, but derailment, this is your project, it's what you're doing already."

Gerrard let out a puff of smoke. He didn't seem to be quite able to figure out that he was receiving an invitation. Natalie's Cyril was just as thickheaded, as stubborn, as Cecile's in *Bonjour.* He started coughing and Guy Debord slapped him on the back, tried to get the smoke out of him. When the cough subsided into sputtering, Guy smiled.

"You've got to remember one thing," he said.

"What?"

"The trick is to create disorder without loving it."

12

The American family in his bookstore was more interested in seeing him, in meeting Christopher Robin Milne, than they were in any of the books. It was difficult to tell the age of their little boy, but he was maybe eight years old, and his parents asked if Chris sold stuffed animals, and helped him search the store for evidence of Edward Bear.

Christopher found a volume of his father's poetry and brought it over for them.

"Don't you have the bear stories?" the father asked.

"They move fast. I need to order more."

"You don't have any copies at all? Nothing?"

"Only my own private copies, and those, of course, are not for sale."

The American considered this. Christopher waited for a bid, sure that this man with his wide-collared suit jacket and his mod wife, whose rust-colored polyester dress was marked with a bright yellow sunflower on her hip, would insult him with their money, but they didn't. Instead they made a different, if still entirely inappropriate, suggestion.

"Would you read one of the stories, from your copy, to my son?"

Christopher stepped back from the counter and raised his hands involuntarily, but the tourist persisted.

"You could read to both of the boys," the American said. He gestured to Daniel, who was sitting in the far corner of the shop, perched Indian style on a step stool. Daniel was counting the books with red covers.

"I don't think so."

"You don't read to your boy?"

Christopher did, of course, read to Daniel, but he did not read children's stories to him. His son couldn't follow even the simplest plot, but wanted to hear about gardening, photosynthesis, and home repair. Christopher had never even considered reading any of his father's stories to Daniel, and would not have done so at this man's suggestion if Daniel had not turned away from counting and taken an interest in the idea himself.

"Story time?" Daniel asked. "Grandfather's stories?"

"No. Not now, Daniel," Chris said. "He doesn't really remember my father."

"I want to hear Grandfather's story time," Daniel said. He carried over two red books, *The Catcher in the Rye* and the *New Testament,* and then sat down heavily in one of the beanbags there.

Christopher realized that to resist this would be more embarrassing than to give in, and he was surprised by Daniel's interest.

The American boy was very quiet. Christopher read from the table of contents of *The House at Pooh Corner* and asked him to pick his favorite, but the boy wouldn't answer him. Instead

Christopher picked out the chapter he wanted to hear. A feeling of recognition, of déjà vu, overtook Chris as he sat in the wooden rocking chair, cleared his throat, and found the correct page from which to begin. Chris read his father's words. He lingered over the strange capitalizations.

" 'It's a Missage,' Edward Bear said to himself, 'that's what it is. It's a very important Missage to me, and I can't read it. I must find Christopher Robin or Owl or Piglet, one of those Clever Readers who can read things, and they will tell me what this missage means. Only I can't swim. Bother!' " Christopher read.

When Christopher reached the end he looked to where he thought the American boy had been, but didn't see him anymore, and the American couple weren't paying attention. Instead of keeping an eye on their son they were examining a coffee table book, an oversized photography book entitled *Moulton's Barn*.

"Excuse me," Christopher said. He looked around the store for the boy and didn't see him anywhere. "Excuse me," he repeated as he got up from his stool.

The couple didn't seem very concerned when Chris approached them. He'd been reading from *The House at Pooh Corner*, just one story, and when he looked up the boy was gone, but rather than helping Chris look the parents just continued flipping through his inventory.

"Sometimes he does that," the father said.

"Sometimes SHE does that," the mother corrected.

"I thought we'd agreed."

"Well, it doesn't matter anymore, does it? And I've always wanted a girl."

Before Christopher could ask any more questions, before he could really figure out what was going on, Daniel intervened.

"The Woodentops are falling down," he yelled.

Chris stepped toward his son, realizing immediately that the boy was about to switch over from his usual routine of counting and echolalia into a full-blown fit. He reached out for Daniel so as to contain him before he started kicking and hitting, before the random violence began, but Daniel stepped out of reach, and Chris fell, sprawling onto the beanbags and orange carpet.

Daniel took off, tearing through the store, knocking the post-card spinner to the ground, smashing into shelves, pulling books down, and then, finally, spitting and kicking, falling to the ground himself.

The Americans were oblivious. "Take a picture, Tom," the wife said. They stood over the scene as Christopher tried to talk Daniel back into his usual state of quiet detachment. Chris spoke to Daniel of railroad schedules, average temperatures, and mentioned the channel numbers on television.

"Twelve and eight and three," Christopher said.

"But eight doesn't show anything. No signal on eight. Just static," Daniel said. "Just static." His arms and legs relaxed. Chris held the boy down and felt the energy of the struggle dissipate.

"That's right. No picture on eight, but only static," Christopher said.

After the scene was over, when Daniel had returned to his stool and resumed counting books, the Americans thanked Christopher for his time, and started to leave.

"Wait a minute," Christopher said. "We need to find your son."

"Our daughter," the father said.

"Either way. Your child has gone missing," Christopher said.

But the Americans demurred. They hadn't had a child really, not a real child. It was actually a personal matter, between the two of them.

"We'll buy that book of poems. Your father's book?" the husband asked. "Will that do?"

"You've been very kind. It was very nice of you to read to her," the wife told him.

Christopher sat on the cement steps built into the hillside that divided Dartmouth. For centuries the town had been constrained by the hillside, split by it. People had built as far as they could at the bottom and then had climbed to solid ground and continued on building. There was a ring of grassy unspoiled hillside, a natural gap that had to be navigated if one was walking from Townstal to a friend who lived above. At least there had been a gap, but now the local council had seen fit to fix the problem, to bridge the gap with concrete steps.

Chris sat halfway up and let his disapproval fester in his stomach. There had been a natural beauty to the empty hillside but now there were steps that made his walk easy and convenient. Sitting there on the cold concrete, listening to the wind, it seemed to Christopher that he didn't understand anything, and without this hillside, without the gap between upper and lower, Chris could scarcely perceive the town at all. He saw his bookstore, the library building, the rows of pretty cottages and lawns, but Dartmouth itself had been obliterated.

Chris had set out that evening in order to get away from Abby and Daniel. The boy always enjoyed his programs, his time with the television, and usually Chris didn't begrudge him this pleasure even if he did not share it with him, but that night Chris had opened the window in the study before switching the picture box on, and the feeling of cool air on his face, the goodness of that breath, made him resent the idea of an hour with the BBC or Eurovision.

Christopher tossed down stones he'd collected. He frequently gathered stones and interesting twigs along with whatever clearly edible mushrooms and roots he might find. He tossed an oval sandstone and watched it bounce down the cement steps.

When Chris had been eight or nine his father had written a poem about him, about little Christopher Robin. The poem was entitled "In the Dark" and it described young Christopher talking to dragons and imagining himself as a pirate, and it culminated with Christopher drifting off into an easy sleep.

The poem had been a lie. While his father described Christopher's time in the dark as another example of how easy it was for Chris to experience innocent and narcissistic pleasure, in reality Christopher had tossed and turned at night for the usual reasons. He could never get comfortable and could never let go of his fear.

Listening to the beat of the bouncing stone, he remembered trying to dance with the first girl with whom he'd ever been romantically involved. He remembered occupied Italy and meeting a girl named Elene.

Chris had been so unsure of himself with her, that while he'd known full well how to move his feet in a waltz, when he got her on the dance floor he hadn't been able to start dancing because he hadn't been able to find the right moment for it. His feet had twitched. He'd moved his right foot forward a bit, and then put it down again, and then stopped. Would she take his cue and move when he did, or would their bodies collide? He'd worried himself into paralysis through the whole song. He hadn't danced to the tune "Honeysuckle Rose."

Chris had been good at building bridges and giving and taking orders during the war, but terrible at dancing.

When he'd been very young he'd dreamt that he was falling. Not that he was falling off a cliff into empty space, but more that he was gliding. . . . Christopher would close his eyes and feel himself slip, feel himself slide down, like he was on a track or like he was being pulled by a string.

His father wrote stories about him, about a Christopher who was always little and silly. But was that how his father really saw him? Was that how his father wanted him to be?

Sitting on the steps Christopher couldn't decide if it was the Americans with their fictional son, the way Dartmouth was changing, or the sale of Cotchford Farm and the destruction of all of his father's personal effects that was causing him to fall. He didn't understand why his father's death made him feel more and more trapped as Christopher Robin.

The last time Christopher had thought he was quite through with stuffed bears and his father's distant judgment was when he'd gone off to Cambridge. He'd thought that while he had not received the tools from his father that he'd needed—he'd gotten nothing to help him make the transition from being the girlish and somewhat dim child of his father's stories and poems into manhood—that he had nonetheless somehow managed to do well enough.

At Cambridge Christopher had purchased a pipe to puff on while working on equations and sums for his courses in applied mathematics, and he'd thought he'd appeared as an adult this way, but soon enough the incompetent schoolboy with long hair and a stuffed bear had returned.

It was a rare thing to find a phonograph player in one of the cottages at Cambridge, but the fellow Christopher shared his bedroom with in 1939 had such a device at his disposal and would play records at all times of day or night. If Chris was studying, or attempting to discuss politics or sport in the sitting room, his roommate would interrupt with the sound of the phonograph needle skipping across a Satie symphony or the crooning of some jazz singer like Bessie Smith or Josephine Baker. However, over time the existence of the phonograph player became less of a nuisance. Christopher became accustomed to it and even able to enjoy the over-proximity of recorded music. It was only after his roommate decided to use the phonograph in order to pull a prank that Christopher had to request a transfer to a different cottage.

Simon Palmer was the boy's name, and he'd gotten ahold of Gracie Fields's recording of "Christopher Robin Is Saying His Prayers," a song that simply lifted his father's poem entitled "Vespers" and set it to music.

The prank was playing the poem twice through while Christopher had company. As it spun Chris's face grew red and then redder still.

"God bless Mummy, I know that's right. God bless, Daddy. I quite forgot."

It wasn't that they'd laughed at him, though they had laughed, but that he himself couldn't distinguish between the little boy saying his prayers to God in the poem and the Christopher who hoped God might see him smoking his pipe and let him finally be an adult. Christopher felt himself to be just as flat as the record and, like the record, etched with grooves and notes that were not of his own making.

13

In January of 1968 the newly constructed swimming pool at Nanterre was opened, and Natalie attended the inauguration ceremony with a plan to intervene. Gerrard stood next to her at the edge of the indoor swimming pool and suggested that they try imagining that the building was a milk bottle. Instead of concrete walls they were behind transparent glass fogged over by the steam rising off the chlorinated blue water. Natalie thought about this, about glass, as she stared into the blue water. She didn't look up until the university president shook hands with François Missoffe, the minister of youth affairs and sport, and started speaking into the microphone.

There were maybe a hundred people attending the ceremony including newspaper reporters, professors, administrators, and students, and all them were bored. The men's and women's swim teams stood in lines of six by the shallow end of the pool. The men were first, nearer to the edge, and the women were behind them. They stood shivering and yawning in black elastane swimsuits. The minister of youth affairs, a skinny middle-aged man with curly grey hair, looked something like a film star, a bit like Paul Meurisse. Confident in his tan cotton trench coat, vest, beige pants, and leather gloves, he coughed politely, removed his gloves and coat, and handed them to the women's swim coach. This middle-aged blond woman in a red and brown and orange track suit took the minister's effects to the bleachers and, after folding the coat and stashing the gloves in the breast pocket, handed them to a younger woman in horn-rimmed glasses.

The minister waited for the university president to finish the introduction, then stepped up to the microphone, adjusted the stand so that it stood higher, aligned the device with his mouth, and then announced that he was pleased.

"This new addition to the University of Nanterre will bring fitness and sport to the students and teachers here. It strikes me as an essential facility, one that is both good for the student body at the university and for the larger body of France," he said. "However, today's university students are so focused on getting ahead in their careers, so determined to make their way to the top of their chosen professions, that they may not feel they have the time for a leisurely swim. It is difficult to predict to what extent these students will find time to use the new facility," he stated. "This is why it is imperative that all students be required to take physical education classes, and specifically to be instructed in effective swimming methods, as a part of their general education course work."

The reason the university put the new pool behind glass, the reason they trapped it in a milk bottle, was because they wanted the students to be bored. Watching the women's swim team stand on the cold concrete, seeing the girls stretch, yawn, and scratch at the edges of their suits, Natalie could feel their power and energy evaporate. The ceremony was constructed, planned

out, to contain the students behind glass, to bottle up the boys
and girls in black swimsuits. The swimming pool suppressed
desire by naming it health.

Natalie was not bored. She wasn't trapped in a milk bottle,
but armed with a hammer.

A boy named Daniel Cohn-Bendit smiled at Natalie. He'd
heard his cue. With his red hair and freckles he looked a bit like
a movie star himself, or like Elvis Presley, and he walked around
the edge of the pool to the minister, slowly and deliberately,
so as not to slip. He was twenty-three years old and probably the
oldest student present. He stepped forward and raised his hand
to interrupt the youth minister, but he did not wait to be called
upon to speak.

"Sir, I understand you've written a book about us?" Daniel
Cohn-Bendit asked.

M. Missoffe tried to continue with his speech about physical
education and personal ambition, to continue his advocacy of
a program for both, his argument of the necessity for both in a
modern capitalist state, but Cohn-Bendit kept on.

"You've written a thick book about youth in France," Cohn-
Bendit said. He turned to look across the pool at the dozen or so
students who were his real audience. "It's about three hundred
pages long?"

"I wrote a book. That's correct. May I continue?"

"I've read your book," Cohn-Bendit said. "It covers quite a
lot of ground, quite a lot about us, about university students, but
you left out the one subject that affects us most." Cohn-Bendit
turned back to face his adversary again. He smiled at the minister, and paused. "You didn't write about the problem of sex."

The minister didn't blink. "You have a problem with sex?"

"Yes, sir. But you never mentioned it in your book. You only hinted at the problem with talk of career and personal drive, in-dividual effort. Sex is an economic issue. Something a girl saves up like a dowry. Something a man purchases like a car, or with a car."

"With your looks I'm not surprised that this is a problem for you," the minister said.

"You would have us channel our natural urges into work, into production, into the state. Your policies of denial, of sup-pression, are fascist."

Natalie knew Cohn-Bendit was an opportunist, but now she was grateful for him, for his audacity.

"If you have such problems with sex that you can't be silent, if you are so inadequate that you must interrupt a public speech marking the occasion of the opening of a swimming pool, but must interject something unrelated—"

Cohn-Bendit gestured toward the swim teams in their semi-nakedness.

"For us the issue is always present. Unrelated? Really?"

"Why don't you jump in the pool to cool off? Go ahead. Sink to the bottom?"

"You want me to jump in?"

"If you are so full of sex problems then you should jump."

"Fascist."

"Child."

They had everything trapped behind glass, had everyone cornered, but Natalie had a hammer. "I'll jump," she said. She stepped forward and pulled her wool sweater off over her head. She unbuttoned her skirt and let it drop. She stripped down to and then out of her underwear, making a point of unhooking and then tossing her bra by the side of the pool like a stripper might do it, with a bit of a flourish, and then she jumped. She grabbed her legs and made a cannonball as she went into the pool. She splashed the minister of youth affairs and Danny Cohn-Bendit both.

When she bobbed back to the surface she saw that Gerrard was undressing too, as were two others from their group, both girls from Natalie's dorm. A fellow student from Gerrard's sociology class, not with Les Détournés but just a spectator, started to undress along with them.

"Everybody in," the sociology student said. He jumped in without taking off his glasses.

In a moment nearly all of the students were in the pool, naked and splashing. The girls' swim team was swimming below the surface like seals.

The newsmen were taking pictures, but they stepped back for a moment in order to protect their cameras.

"This is finished," the minister said.

"I concur," Cohn-Bendit said. He was the only student still fully dressed and dry. "It is finished for certain."

14

O n March 22, 1968, there were about a hundred or so of
them huddled underneath the glass awning on the north
side of the administration building and Daniel Cohn-Bendit
spoke there in front of the double doors. He said the building
represented the omnipresent eye of the university bureaucracy,
that the stench of the university system was so overwhelming
that the students could no longer take part, that they could no
longer even passively take part. But before he'd finished the
students from Les Détournés pushed past him and opened the
doors.

This was how they occupied the building: The doors weren't
locked so they just walked in.

Gerrard sat next to Natalie on the tile floor on the fourth
level. He leaned over to her and showed her a detourned Luc
Orient comic that he'd been working on. The comic was originally titled *The Secret of the 7 Lights,* and Gerrard didn't change
this, but the adventure plot had been replaced with metaphysi-
cal talk about dreams. The hero Luc Orient argued with his

girlfriend Lora and his mentor, the Indian professor Hugo Kala, about whether they could watch their lives on television.

"There should be no delay between what we do and what appears on the screen," Luc said.

The three characters were studying a color television set where the picture hadn't quite come in. The device was only picking up abstractions, and Lora objected.

"If we watch our lives in real time then nothing can happen," she said. "It's just a regress."

Luc Orient looked puzzled inside the comic book frame.

Natalie didn't see the point of his derailed version of the comic, but she had to admit that Gerrard had been taking Debord's instruction to derail his studies to heart. Natalie never saw Gerrard in class anymore, but had met up with him a few times at the library. Gerrard spent hours there altering newspapers and cutting up magazines.

Gerrard caught Natalie's hand and pulled her close.

"What happened to your friend with the Citroën convertible?" he asked.

"She feels it isn't ethical," Natalie said. She scooted away from Gerrard and then stood up and tried to find a better conversation than the one she'd just read between Luc Orient and Lora, but ended up with philosophy students who were debating Hegel, which was pretty much just the same conversation again. Gerrard followed her anyhow. He stood next to her and listened to the conversation for a moment before offering his opinion.

"Everybody has a double consciousness," Gerrard said. He looked sane and calm, but he went on. "It's probably because we're all cartoon characters reading about ourselves and our adventures with Tintin."

Natalie was tired of his game, and when they occupied a

conference hall on the eighth floor she tried to find a place to sit where there wouldn't be room for Gerrard. She squeezed in next to a young man in a rumpled trench coat and a sweater vest. He seemed surprised that Natalie wanted to sit right up next to him. She squeezed in between him and the bench's armrest, but this was all to no avail because Gerrard just sat in the aisle. He started humming and then softly singing a pop song to himself, under his breath. Gerrard was off key as he sang Johnny Hallyday's song "Smoke Covers My Eyes."

"All changes into dream now," he sang. "I remain there."

Natalie was pretty sure she didn't want Gerrard anymore. Her friends in Les Détournés felt that he was unstable, untrustworthy, and worse, while Debord had seemed to sanction him, Natalie no longer saw how he fit in with her project. Derailing Sagan's book, living it, was about realizing the goal of free love. As bad as it was to read the book, living it was a way to realizing the philosophy it contained, but there was nothing free about sleeping with Gerrard. Being Gerrard's lover came with a price.

She'd dreamt of Gerrard in New York City and in her dream they'd been living together in an art deco loft, an uncluttered space, modern and clean. They were newly married and Natalie was alone in their new home. She walked up the stairs from their minimalist off-white living room with wall-to-wall carpeting and an off-white vinyl sofa to a sunlit bedroom that contained a flat white mattress and nothing more. She crossed the bedroom and found a bathroom with a silver-walled shower already filled with steam. The knobs for the hot and cold water were made of glass.

After bathing she wrapped a white towel around her body and stepped back into the nearly empty bedroom. The room was cool, air conditioned, and when she let the towel fall away her body felt cold.

Next thing she knew she was with Gerrard and they were eating ice cream together in front of a perfectly white refrigerator. She took a spoon and worked out a frozen bite, and was disappointed that the ice cream didn't taste like anything. He'd promised her oranges and cream and instead she was eating something blank. It was nothing. And when she woke up she couldn't shake the feeling that she was still there, still in America. Even worse, the dream had made her orgasm. The tasteless American ice cream had made her climax.

Gerrard was still talking to the philosophy students and she wanted him to stop, but Gerrard didn't look at her. Finally she leaned over to him and whispered in his ear.

"Shut up, please," she said. "Shhhh!"

One of Natalie's friends, a boy named Rene, stepped up to the lectern. He was tall and neatly dressed, his blond hair perfectly combed, and he held his curled fingers up to his eyes, seeming to inspect his cuticles, and then cleared his throat.

"Les Détournés cannot find common ground with Stalinists." Natalie agreed as the cute boy suggested that the five or so known Stalinists should leave. He said it coolly, with a nonchalant indifference, and it was just right that way.

But Daniel Cohn-Bendit stepped up next to him at the podium, his unruly red hair and freckled face looked coarse when juxtaposed against the face and hair of the ultra-leftist. Still Cohn-Bendit smiled at the Les Détournés member, nodded as if to agree, and then waved his left hand over the crowd. Cohn-Bendit appeared to be blessing the students in the first row.

"Those who were Stalinists are no longer Stalinist," Cohn-Bendit said.

"What?" the Les Détournés member sputtered.

"We've transcended those divisions and usual ideologies."

"How did we do that?" the cute boy asked him. "Just a moment. The Stalinists should leave. If they won't leave we will."

"Those who were Stalinists are no longer Stalinist," Danny said again. He smiled and smiled as the Les Détournés members in the audience started to move. Natalie stood up too, but wondered at how the group had moved from interrupting professors to disrupting the occupation. Still, she stood up to join her friends, and Gerrard started to stand up also.

Natalie turned to him. "Stay," she said.

"What?"

"We're through," she said. "You and I are finished. There is too much going on, too many important things."

Gerrard looked at her, but didn't respond.

"I can't afford to be confused right now. So just stay here. I'm leaving and you're staying."

When Natalie went to join her friends in the hall she found that most of them were just sort of standing there waiting. One boy in blue jeans was carrying a guitar case and he looked disappointed.

"Had you been expecting to play?" Natalie asked him. He started to tell her about finger-style jazz and why it was radical, but Natalie lost interest quickly. Standing in the hall with nothing to do now, they'd exiled themselves.

Natalie looked back, turned, and opened the swinging door to the auditorium, and saw that Gerrard was still sitting in the aisle. He had his legs crossed and he sort of looked like he might be paying attention to what Cohn-Bendit was saying.

Natalie watched him for a moment more, wondering if he'd turn around and catch her looking.

15

Gerrard thought of Christopher Robin while he waited for the Metro train that would take him back home to Ménilmontant. He looked into the darkness to the west, at the dim red lights on the sooty wall, spaced at regular intervals and disappearing along the curve, and tried to think about Natalie instead. Simple heartbreak was a pleasure for him. It was like something out of a movie. If he concentrated he could still imagine himself at the centre of a romance, the lonely hero waiting for the train after losing the girl.

This was how he wanted to see himself, how he wanted to direct his thoughts, but after a few minutes of waiting, after enough time had passed for the scene to be mundane rather than romantic, his thoughts drifted away from Natalie with her short blond hair and bright brown eyes and onto the general pattern of his life. He remembered one embarrassment after another, like how he'd had a bloody nose in his fourth year of primary school.

He remembered turning in an algebra test splattered with blots of blood. The teacher had chastised him. She'd told him not to pick his nose in class, and made him stand at the front of the class with his finger in his nostril. The fact that he was guilty only made his punishment worse.

Gerrard was in the wrong book. He didn't want to be in *Bonjour Tristesse* or *Luc Orient,* but in *The House at Pooh Corner.* He'd derailed the wrong narrative. The Metro train pulled up to him on the platform and he stepped onboard, put his suitcase down, and looked for a place to sit. He looked at each passenger, tried to catch each person's gaze, but not one of them would look at him. The businessman in a thin tie and black blazer had slicked-back hair and a blank gaze that made him seem somewhat dangerous, while the blond girl in a modish checkered dress beside him had a face that seemed soft, but this only indicated how young she was in comparison to the middle-aged man she was with. She had been crying and she was looking down at her expensive shoes.

An old man across from him, a man with a receding hairline, white wisps above wire-rimmed glasses, whose flannel shirt was neatly pressed and clean, was the only one who reacted to Gerrard's presence. The man's eyes focused in on Gerrard, and he seemed to want to say something, but could not quite manage it. The man sat perfectly still, with a paper shopping bag between his knees, and stared at him.

"What is it?" Gerrard asked.

"You're too young to know," the old man said. "But there was a war. There was an occupation." The old man took off his glasses and looked out into the dark, at the cement walls of the Metro tunnel. The old man had a black kerchief around his neck, and his trench coat was too big for him. He'd shrunk since he originally purchased the coat. "I've lived too long," the man said. And Gerrard realized that the man was speaking in English.

Gerrard turned away from the old man. He didn't want to look at him. Instead he tried to remember his father, to remember what his father had looked like, or the sound of his voice, but ended up thinking of Christopher Robin Milne and his toys instead. Gerrard remembered Milne's stuffed animals, thought of a Hundred Acre Wood, a boy, and his bear. Gerrard remembered a photograph of the stuffed animals. They'd been put on display in a publishing house in New York City after touring America. He'd been six or seven at the time, and he'd cut a photograph of the toys out of a copy of *Paris Match* and hung the photo over his small bed.

The train moved along, clicking on the tracks. Gerrard was no longer sure if the old man was French or British, or if the old man had ever spoken at all. Gerrard looked out his own window, at the grey cement outside, then held his nose closed and looked at his watch. Until he looked down at it, he hadn't even realized he was wearing a watch. Two minutes went by like that, and the train stayed in the tunnel. The same graffiti slogan about liberating humanity came into view again and then passed.

Gerrard thought again about Christopher Robin Milne, about the way he and his bear would always be in the Hundred Acre Wood, and how they would always be playing. In one of the stories Christopher Robin had been a knight or a king. He had made the bear promise always to remember him, even if he changed, even when he was a hundred.

Christopher Robin had lived through World War 2. Gerrard remembered reading that Christopher had been a soldier in that war. The boy from those stories had probably seen death up close. On the battlefield of history Christopher Robin had seen how it all goes, how everything ends. Gerrard looked at his watch and continued to hold his breath. He counted in his head: ten more seconds, and then twenty more on top of that.

Christopher Robin owned a bookstore in England. Gerrard had read that somewhere. He was probably married and probably owned a color television set.

Gerrard took his suitcase out from under his seat and opened it up on his lap. He removed a black-and-white composition notebook and a fountain pen from the inside pocket, and then closed the suitcase and left it in his lap. He started writing to Christopher Robin during that train ride. He looked up at the woman in the checkered dress and winked at her. Gerrard held his breath as he wrote and didn't mind when the text shifted around on him:

"The vacuum cleaner in your bookstore, and the fresh air in the orange carpet, is nothing but what you find inside. The television is a woman who knows nothing but war. The television is in your bed."

Christopher Robin Milne was a soldier in World War 2 and had seen the centre of his life blown away. What he needed, Gerrard realized, was to be reminded of the simple pleasure of doing nothing, of listening to all the things that he couldn't hear, and seeing all the things that weren't there. He needed, Gerrard decided, to be reminded how to be friends with a bear.

"Doing nothing is my favorite thing to do," the old man in the trench coat said. Gerrard couldn't tell if he was speaking French or English, but just opened his notebook, turned the page, and started again.

Gerrard wrote down the words: "Dear Billy Moon."

16

After he'd read the letter from Gerrard, Christopher couldn't sleep. It was a warm night in late April, 1968, and Chris stripped down to his boxers and climbed into bed with Abby. She'd kicked off their checkered quilt and her nightgown had drifted up, exposing her hip. Christopher stopped to look, to pet her auburn hair before lying next to her and pulling up the quilt. Half-asleep, she reached over, stroked his cheek, and tousled his hair. Then Christopher turned onto his side, faced away from her, and stared at the time. He watched his Tymeter clock radio spin the seconds away. Sometimes, especially when he couldn't sleep, it seemed his life was a mechanism just like a clock, a clock that ran anticlockwise. Christopher listened to Abby's breathing, waited until he was sure she was fully asleep, and then sat up and turned on the radio part of the device. When he turned the dial, the first station to come in clearly was playing the sort of light pop music he couldn't stand. He was thinking of trying his luck down the dial when Daniel opened the door and climbed up on the bed, crawled across his parents, and found a place across the width of the bottom of the bed.

Christopher turned off the clock radio, waited for Daniel to settle back into sleep, then got out of bed and quietly crossed the wood floor, steadying himself with his left hand on the rough stone wall of the farmhouse.

They'd been in the house since 1966, but Christopher still missed living above the bookshop. On Fairflax Place his insomnia had some usefulness. He'd crept downstairs and rearranged the books on their shelves, or filled out purchase orders, but now he was awake and there was nothing to do but wait for sleep.

Christopher's feet were bare and the coolness from the stones crept into his hand and down his arm. He fetched a pair of slippers and a terrycloth robe, opened his closet door and removed a cardboard box, then made his way to the kitchen where he cracked a tin of biscuits, took the foil off a bottle of milk, and sat down at the kitchen island.

Disappointed to discover the shortbread biscuits were gone, he dipped dry bourbons into his milk and then moved the whole operation to the study where they kept another radio. This slightly larger wooden box had a flip top glass station indicator that Christopher could operate with ease, but when he tuned in his favorite station he found the 1910 Fruitgum Company still singing their mindless pop hit, or singing it all over again.

"The name of the game is Simple Simon Says, and I'd like for you to play it too," Mark Gutkowski, the lead singer of Fruitgum, explained to Chris. Then, halfway through, the needle was lifted from the groove and another record placed on the radio station's turntable. Françoise Hardy's "It Hurts to Say Goodbye" filled the gap left by the interruption, and Christopher decided he had tuned in the wrong station.

It was three in the morning and Christopher sat in his study listening to a young woman singing light pop in French. He opened the cardboard box and took each item out and placed it on the kitchen table. He put the Merrythought cat down first, then the broken Piglet doll, then the jar of mud, the orange poster, a copy of *Bonjour Tristesse,* a Munchies wrapper, and now this letter from a boy named Gerrard Hand. Sitting in the plush brown leather chair in his study and looking it over Christopher felt small; he felt like a child. He tried to find something else on the radio, but there was nothing for him. There was no Beethoven, no Bach. Nothing to be found either up or down the dial.

Christopher no longer wanted to sleep. He refused to give in to sleep. Instead he returned to the kitchen and made himself a cup of black tea and ate another stale bourbon biscuit. He parked himself at the kitchen table and looked at each item again. He wondered if the Munchies wrapper really belonged with the other items, but couldn't bring himself to finally throw it away.

Since he wasn't going to sleep Chris went over the books from the bookstore. And he decided he should stop carrying secondhand books. That was the economically sound decision. Customers who wanted secondhand books weren't readers in any case, they were collectors, and as such were an entirely different breed from his usual patrons. All that concerned buyers of secondhand books was the price. It took too much energy out of him and ultimately wasn't worth the effort to close the sale.

He'd had to deal with the problem that morning. An old man had wanted Christopher to knock a full pound off the price of six books, and the man's face had turned red when Christopher refused. He wouldn't lower and the man made as if to walk out of the shop, but he'd turned back.

Christopher had followed the man out, patted him on the

back, and wished him well. He'd opened the door for the collector, and that was when he'd spotted the morning's mail. The letter had been sitting on the mat right inside the entrance.

It started out in English but drifted into French as it went along. It began as an invitation and ended up a paranoid accusation.

Christopher had received scores of fan letters since he'd opened the bookshop. Six-year-olds wrote him to ask about his bear. Adults who'd read his father's books when they were young wrote to ask the same questions. Everyone wanted pretty much the same thing, and Christopher couldn't give any answers. He didn't know how to find the Hundred Acre Wood, and he didn't know where childhood went to over the years, or why it was so difficult to feel real joy. He threw almost all of these letters away because they weren't for him at all, but were really addressed to a boy Christopher's father had made up.

His father had written Christopher to serve as a comic foil for animal characters that were defined by their faults. He played straight man to an empty-headed bear, a pessimistic donkey, a self-aggrandizing rabbit, but as a foil Christopher always shared commonalities with the characters he played against.

Christopher Robin the character was a great success, but the real Christopher was not. It wasn't so much that Chris had disappointed or failed to live up to expectations, but his existence undermined the world his father had built around himself, the artificial world of his reputation and his stories. As a reminder of A. A. Milne's own lost youth and worse, a reminder of the unpredictable and unknowable outside world that the older Milne had worked so hard to avoid, Christopher was an embarrassment.

"Despite everything," the letter writer had dared to assert, "you miss your father. You won't find him in Dartmouth, and there is nothing left of him on the farm."

Christopher returned to bed, lay down again, and when he shut his eyes his mind conjured up Heffalumps. His wife and son breathed deeply and peacefully, but he was kept from sleep by Technicolor images: pink and purple elephants, cartoons from the Hollywood version of his father's books. Chris couldn't keep the Heffalumps away; he couldn't stop thinking or dreaming of Woozles.

"If you want to escape him you'll have to find him again. You'll need to find something of what he made for you, what he made of you," the letter writer had written in French.

"The bear is waiting for you."

Daniel especially loved the sailboats, loved to say the word *sailboat* whether or not there were any there at all, though there usually were a few. From the bookstore window Daniel and Christopher would count the sails.

"Sailboat, sailboat, sailboat."

It was May 3, 1968, and Chris was scheduled to fly to Paris. He woke Daniel early, helped the boy dress in his hiking shorts, red-and-black flannel shirt, and boots. Daniel wore the same basic outfit every day, he needed these sorts of consistencies and routines, and for Christopher it was an easy thing to accommodate him, second nature.

The bookstore could open late as business was unseasonably slow. They left Abby to sleep in, opened the front door, and stepped onto the boardwalk. Dartmouth was as pleasant a place to walk as Cotchford Farm ever was. They breathed in the moist air, inhaled the smell of ocean, and looked out at the green hills on the other side of the River Dart. Chris felt good listening to the water, smelling the green hills, and even though Daniel gave no indication of any change, Chris felt sure that he too was moved. Chris pointed to houses that had been built in the Middle Ages and tried to teach him the words *wattle* and *daub*. When Daniel spotted a sailboat, Chris reminded him that the port had once been a favorite for pirates and other notorious seamen.

Every couple of yards Daniel stopped to fetch a stone and then, with great effort, send it flying over the boardwalk and into the river.

"This is the story about the Woodentops," Daniel said. The Woodentops were from the television.

"Can you see Dartmouth Castle?" Chris asked. He pointed it out to Daniel; it sat across the river to the south.

"There was Mama Woodentop and the baby, and Daddy Woodentop, and Willie."

Daniel's symptomatic way of talking, his delayed echolalia, was not usually communicative, but it could be. Sometimes Daniel would offer up a quote from the Roundabout as a comment on what was going on around them, or he would use these involuntary utterances to call attention to himself. Chris usually continued on as though Daniel hadn't spoken at all, but the meaning of what he was saying was obvious and it almost felt as though they were having a conversation.

"I'm leaving Dartmouth today. You and your mum will run the shop for me while I'm in Paris. Do you remember? I told you about Paris? I'm going to fly there on a jet plane."

Daniel picked up another rock and dropped it over the side.

"This is the story about the Woodentops," Daniel said again.

"There was Mommy Woodentop and the baby, and last of all the very biggest spotty dog you ever did see." Daniel stopped at the water's edge, leaned down to put his fingers in the water, lay down on the wooden slats, and dangled his arms over the side. Splashing around he looked like nothing other than a normal seven-year old, and Chris felt guilty for the warm feeling that surged in his chest. Why should he love the boy more when he looked normal?

Chris lay down next to his son, dangled his own arms off the side in the same way, let his fingers skirt across the top of the water, and felt the flow.

"I won't be gone for too long, maybe a week. Your mother will take care of you."

"Every government has its Secret Service branch," Daniel said again. "America, CIA; France, Deuxième Bureau; England, MI5."

"Don't worry. Your mum has it all down and I'll be back before you know it."

"This is the story of the Woodentops," Daniel said.

"That's right."

The river was bigger, more permanent than they were, and indifferent to them and their condition. Chris felt the cool water of the Dart, thought about how many had dipped their hands in the same water, about Chaucer's shipman and the years of piracy, the years of civil war. He glanced across the water and stared at the other bank, at the brown dirt and tall grass on the other side.

"Nothing can ever, could ever, change," Chris said. Then he stood up, abruptly displeased with himself, with the situation.

"This is the story of the Woodentops. The CIA, Deuxième Bureau, and MI5."

"I'll be just a little while. You'll be fine. You'll be fine," Chris said. "I'll be back soon, son."

Christopher stirred his Coca-Cola with the thin green straw the stewardess had given him. With his seat in an upright position and his tray down he was aware of how small the space he occupied actually was, and how impossible it was.

He stirred the cola with the straw but this had no effect. The liquid content of his plastic cup was fixed, perfectly balanced, homeostatic. Sunlight streamed in through the Plexiglas pane in the porthole. The sunlight made his beverage glow orange and brown. Moving the straw through the liquid, he had a sense that the moment was open, that it was easy to push against it, but when he considered where he was, when he thought of the empty space, the air outside, the impossibility of flight, he realized that the ease he felt was illusory.

He'd told Abby that there was a mystery he was trying to solve. The letter writer from Paris had known details from Chris's life that nobody should or could have known. For instance, the letter had described what had happened when Christopher had been ordered to climb a water tower and retrieve the corpse of a gunner tangled in the metal access ladder. The body had grown stiff, the man's twisted legs caught between the rungs and, of course, trying to move him ended up compromising the body's physical integrity. His chest split open and Chris was confronted with the fluids any person's body contains along with the sort of rotten liquid that could only obtain after death. Chris had been overwhelmed by the stench, and by the texture of the man's cold limbs.

Abby didn't understand why Chris would be interested in French politics or just what the students at the Sorbonne were on about. Why would he mix himself up in all of that? But Chris told her that the letter writer had known how it felt to survive the war. The guilt involved and the godlessness that lurked behind survival. The war was a random and heartless event and while there had been reasons for it, good reasons, none of them could obscure the fact that every specific act of violence, every death, was without purpose or meaning.

Christopher admitted the answer to the question of how some French student radical might have come across obscure biographical details was not what he wanted. That wasn't why he was going. He'd struggled to find his place in the war and before that, when he'd gone to university, he'd also been out of place whereas his father had never had such difficulties.

When Alan had been a child of eighteen his friend, the editor of *The Elizabethan,* suggested that he should like to edit the journal *Granta* out of Cambridge and Alan had agreed. He'd replied that he would, in fact, edit *Granta*. This is how he left Westminster and how he came to be a writer of some importance. He had simply made a decision.

Christopher, on the other hand, was too aware of all the impossibilities. For instance, the porthole in the airplane gave just one view of a world that could never be seen all at once and Christopher had never found a way to decide.

After receiving the French fan letter, after the exhortation to join in, Abby had been curious about what was happening in Paris. She'd searched out the story, such as it was, from copies of the *International Herald Tribune* and the *Times,* both of which were available at the Devon grocery. She'd told him about the swimming pool disruption, about how students at Nanterre and not in Paris were causing trouble. They were young men who had been told they had nowhere fixed to go to, there was very little room for them in the new French economy.

"But they've acted," Chris said. "They've made a decision."

17

At the Sorbonne Christopher found a pleasant café with sidewalk tables and red-white-and-blue-striped umbrellas right across the street from the exasperated students who were organizing a situation. On May 2 Daniel Cohn-Bendit had been suspended from Nanterre in a disciplinary hearing for the actions of March 22 and on that same day the student union hall was burned down. Dean Grappin had appeared on television to announce that he was shutting down the campus; the students' response was transpiring as Christopher waited for his drink. Cohn-Bendit, for example, arrived with his megaphone right at precisely the same time as Christopher's mimosa, and Chris found it difficult to figure out how many francs he owed while trying to follow what Cohn-Bendit was saying. Chris's French was pretty rusty, and Cohn-Bendit's words were somewhat distorted.

Chris drank his breakfast cocktail and watched. His stomach was empty and he thought of ordering some tea to offset the effect of the champagne, but when the waiter came around again he settled for a small cup of thick coffee. Chris glanced up at the Sorbonne tower, at the dome, and then down again at the students on the street. The baroque backdrop for the struggle, the Sorbonne with its columns and ornamental statues, the majesty of the institution they were opposing, this seemed to work to the students' advantage. After all, rebellions and strikes had occurred many, many times since the first revolution. Why not again? Somehow the Sorbonne made its history visible, the past visible right on the surface of the marble façade, and this made change seem possible.

The students all looked quite smart. The boys had short hair and wore sports jackets and ties while the girls had long hair and wore skirts and dresses. Chris wondered which of them was Gerrard Hand. He wondered what was keeping him.

The table Christopher was sitting at was grooved. There were pictures of animals—of snakes and ducks and lizards and owls—engraved into the uneven surface of the marble, and someone had left a copy of a pamphlet entitled "On the Poverty of Student Life" on the chair next to his. Chris let his coffee grow cold as he worked out the French text. "To transform the world and to change the structure of life are one and the same thing for the proletariat. For the proletariat revolt is a festival or it is nothing."

Chris wasn't sure if he was reading it correctly. He didn't see a clear connection between the first and second sentences. He took the letter Gerrard had written from the inside pocket of his tweed jacket and separated out the altered newspaper advertisement he'd been sent from the letter itself.

Disney and Slesinger had managed to make his father's books into cartoon movies in America and one of the advertisements for these, an advertisement for the first film entitled *Winnie the*

Pooh and the Honey Tree, featured Pooh standing in front of a full-length mirror with his stubby arms over his eyes. Gerrard had rubbed out the original text below the drawing and replaced them with French.

"All that was directly lived has receded into a representation." In this context the bear could be seen to be covering his eyes because he did not want to see his reflection.

Another student now had the bullhorn. She was shouting something about Nanterre, but to Chris it seemed that they were protesting everything. They had signs against racial discrimination, against the Vietnam War, against work, against the "education industry." Somebody had written, in English, that the workers should put their "bodies on the gears and on the wheels, and make it stop." The students protested everything, wanted everything. One of the students held a sign that read, "It is forbidden to forbid."

Was the message meant to be strident or absurd? He remembered a line, a joke, from one of his father's books: "Did you ever stop to think and forget to start again?" He was talking to nobody but himself. "This is not a pipe." Chris spoke the words aloud into the air. It was something he'd seen on a painting by a Belgian named Magritte, a commercial artist who, after designing wallpaper, found his way into the museums by using slick realism to create surreal questions in paintings. Chris had seen the picture of a pipe in the Arts section of the *Times*. The painting of a pipe that was not a pipe was titled "The Treachery of Images."

The painting had not impressed Chris, but he saw that it was clever. The only reason he remembered it was because he'd happened to read the accompanying article that claimed, cleverly or not, that the man responsible, René Magritte, was a surrealist,

and that surrealism was a reaction to the horrors of war, specifically a reaction to the horror of the Great War. It was the machine gun and, in the case of Magritte, the Rape of Belgium that
caused the pipe to abandon its image and the image to abandon
its pipe. The world could no longer be painted; the pipe was not
a pipe. After the Great War there had been nothing left in Europe but this feeling of being disconnected, and this is what
Magritte hoped to transfer onto his canvases, like burning tubas
or giant green apples.

"This is not a pipe." Chris said it again.

On the other side of Boulevard Saint-Michel the police arrived in their kepis. They marched into the square and Chris
nearly spat. It was unreal. The police tossed tear gas grenades
into the crowd. Rather than disperse the students the attack
caused their numbers to swell. Where were these boys and girls
coming from? And more to the point, why? Modern Europe was
a candy-coated pill and all they had to do was swallow it. Why
all this? It made no sense. There had been real problems maybe,
the conflict in French Algeria had taken a toll on French confidence for instance, but these students would have been mere
children when that conflict ended. Yes, the American adventure
in Vietnam was surely terrible, but that didn't seem reason
enough. And yet it was happening, the police were bloodying
the lot of them, and they weren't budging.

Perhaps it was as they claimed, they were tired of sugar pills.
Having been sold versions of themselves, having read about
their fictional counterparts in magazines and books, seen themselves misrepresented in theaters and on television screens, they
no longer could stand the charade.

Chris couldn't keep to himself through it. His body jerked
involuntarily as one of the police struck a young man who wore

round glasses and a fisherman's cap. Chris found himself on his feet and moving before he actually decided to respond. A policeman used his billy club on the lad's back, pushed the student's face down onto the cobblestone with the toe of his boot on the back of the boy's head. Chris pushed his way through, past a few girls in wool sweaters, under the placards and black flags, through the tear gas. He crouched behind a uniformed policeman, reached forward with both hands, grabbed the man's ankles, and then proceeded to pull the policeman's legs out from under him. Chris dragged the cop back several feet from the student before two more officers arrived.

Chris was acting like an idiot, he realized, by attacking an officer. He tried to make things right, to apologize, but other police started in hitting him. This caused him to feel doubly foolish, of course, and then he was angry. They were putting too much strength into it. When Christopher's face hit the cobblestones he tried to complain in his best French, but his mouth was full of blood, his brain shaken, and everything came out in garbled English.

"We can't all," Chris said as the two officers hauled him to his feet and proceeded to march him toward the police van. "We can't all, and some of us don't," he explained.

Gerrard found Christopher Robin in a jail cell underneath the police museum. The storybook character had a bag of ice wrapped in a green cotton towel, and he was pressing it against the wound over his left ear. It had taken Gerrard several hours to recognize him, to figure out that this middle-aged man who spoke halting French through a posh British accent was Christopher Robin, but once he was sure of the fact, Gerrard didn't hesitate to introduce himself. He checked his pockets, found three paper drinking straws, and then laid them down on the wool blanket between them. The straws had red and green stripes up and down the side. Gerrard made a V shape with two of them and then laid the third across the angle.

"You recognize this?" Gerrard asked.

"Drinking straws."

"These are just three straws to you, but to the truly educated these are a great deal more," Gerrard said.

"They are formed into the letter A," Christopher said. It was a reference from one of the stories. The owl had shown the others the letter A made from sticks.

Gerrard smiled. "The letter A. That's right," he said. He opened his mouth to say something more, and then closed it again when he spotted three girls congregated at the bars of the cell across from their own. They were watching him. Gerrard stood up and pressed his face against the bars to talk to the blonde.

"Do you have a 2CV convertible, Mademoiselle?" Gerrard asked.

"Yes, sir. Why do you ask?"

"Where is Natalie?"

"You're Gerrard? Natalie told me that she isn't seeing you anymore."

Gerrard could feel Christopher growing impatient behind him. He heard him coughing and shifting on the cot, but he couldn't help himself. He wanted to find out about Natalie.

"You're a Catholic, right? You disapprove of me?"

"I'm not a Catholic anymore," the girl said. "I'm a revolutionary." She smiled again. They were all of them smiling and smiling. The blond girl pulled her long hair back, put her finger to her bottom lip as if to think, and then she shook her head no and smiled again.

Christopher tapped Gerrard on his shoulder. "You're Gerrard?" Christopher asked.

Gerrard looked at the three drinking straws on the green blanket. Sunlight came into the cell through the barred window and created lines of shadow on the cement floor. There were lines on Christopher's face, frown lines.

"I'd like to know why you . . . that is, what is it that I'm expected to do for you exactly?" Chris asked.

The point of derailing Christopher Robin, of cutting him out of Devon and pasting him down under the police museum, was to use him to disrupt Paris. He was a weapon in a battle that had seemingly been indefinitely postponed but had finally arrived.

Chris was a fake person and this was how he could help. Gerrard tried to explain it to him, to tell him how the Hundred Acre Wood was always waiting for him, to tell him about dreaming and how the past was inside the present, but he kept having to start over.

"This isn't just about you or me. It's like those straws," Gerrard said.

"It is?"

"They're just three stupid straws unless you know how to read them, unless you know that they make the letter A, and once you know it's A you can't unknow it. You're here to show people a new letter A."

"That's very French," Chris said. "Which is to say, I don't have the first idea of what you're talking about."

"Listen, you know why I wrote to you. You are Christopher Robin," Gerrard said.

"I'm not. Those books you've read aren't, were never, about

me," Chris said. He peeled the blood-soaked green towel away from his skin and looked at the clot in the folds of terry cloth, the pool of dried blood there. Then he shifted the towel, found a clean patch, and put the towel back on the wound.

"Why should I take you seriously?" Christopher asked.

This made Gerrard laugh. Not derisive laughter, but as if he'd figured something out, and was pleased to know something.

"You already take me seriously," Gerrard said. "After all, you're already here."

18

When the painter Donald Berreby approached her at the Café Charbon, Natalie let him pick her up. She'd been testing reality while Guy Debord whinged on the failure of the students to grasp the totality of their circumstances, and she'd been watching Alice Becker Ho touch Debord's neck, soothing him. Natalie watched Alice and noted her jealousy. She could cite the page numbers in *Bonjour Tristesse* where Cecile was shown to be jealous, and there were many. Natalie even knew why Cecile was jealous. She turned to page forty-five, found the fourth paragraph, and read the final line:

> *We are all three on the terrace, full of unspoken thoughts, of secret fears, and of happiness.*

Natalie held her nose closed, held her mouth shut, and was silently counting when Donald Berreby approached her. He sat down across from her and told her that she was beautiful. It wasn't a come-on, he explained, just a fact. Another fact was

that Donald required a beautiful companion to help him celebrate.

He pointed to Debord, who was frowning and drawing on
a napkin, and then said it again, loudly, so that Debord could
hear.

"I need a beautiful companion so I can celebrate our victories!"

Guy glanced toward Donald, and then turned back to the
debate at his table.

Natalie left with Donald, who promised to take her to Café de
Flore for gin and across the street to Les Deux Magots for burgundy. Donald Berreby was a British painter who had fallen out
of favor with Debord and his gang a decade earlier. He was a
known quantity. Old like Debord, but tall and good-looking,
with straight black hair and bright eyes. She found him appealing in his perfectly pressed plaid shirt and blue jeans.

"Tonight we should enjoy what the wealthy enjoy, and see if
we can taste the difference," Donald said. He took Natalie by
her arm; as they stepped out onto the street she wondered if she
was participating in a charade. Berreby's face was inscrutable.
Once he was out on the street he moved with purpose, swept her
along, but he stopped looking at her.

Standing in the street with his tan wool trench coat tossed
over his shoulder he seemed impressive. He was even a little like
Sagan's Cyril who was "tall and almost beautiful with the kind
of good looks that inspires one with confidence" even if he cap-
sized his little sailboat or, as was the case, took you to his friend's
apartment on Saint-Germain so that you could change out of
what he called your proletariat house dress and into something
more elegant.

The apartment belonged to a former friend of the Wright
family, and while the apartment was on the top floor and had

low ceilings, it was decorated superbly with an Empire chandelier, tapestries, and an ornate vanity table.

"I think you would look good in red," Donald told her. "For myself, I'll simply find a tie."

Natalie stepped into the bathroom to change, grabbed the shower curtain to steady herself, and almost pulled the curtain down. She was already drunk. She managed to unbutton her blouse and remove it and then to turn on the shower so she could lean into the spray, but when she looked back at where she'd propped her paperback copy of *Tristesse* she saw that it had fallen from the edge of the tub. She picked it up and set it in the sink. Then she leaned back into the shower. She kept her hair dry, swallowed rust-colored water, turned the water off, and removed her skirt. Then she stood there, steadying herself, while considering what to do next.

She wondered how she should react to a strange man dressing her, but her manual was swollen with water damage. She went ahead and slipped into the red velvet evening gown and then looked at herself in the mirror again. The gown was very lovely and fine and she felt confident in it. She adjusted her hair with her hands, slipped her high-heeled sandal-toed shoes back on her bare feet. She took her paperback, shook it over the sink, and then held it gingerly in her left hand and opened the bathroom door with her right. Donald was outside the door waiting for her. Under his arm he held a painting that he was going to bring with them to the Café de Flore. A patron had agreed to meet him there. He would pick up some francs that way, and then he would buy Natalie, the beautiful woman who'd agreed to accompany him, a shot of the best burgundy in Paris.

Donald held the painting out to her for inspection, and Natalie thought of those children's game books with mazes and connect-the-dots puzzles. It turned out that the painting was entitled "The Connections."

"Just some lines," she said.

"Very observant. Thank you. Are you thirsty?"

Once at the café, they found a table, and Donald left her to sit by herself while he looked for his patron who wanted the painting. After what seemed to Natalie a long time but was probably only a few minutes, he came back to their table with a fistful of francs. Natalie asked the waiter to fill a porcelain coffee cup with gin, while Donald ordered a bottle of Pinot noir. The gin was smooth and easy to swallow, but Natalie couldn't be sure whether this reflected an improvement in the quality of the gin or not. The fourth cup of gin was always easier than the first few. She took another sip and then felt something at the top of her head, a tingle. She put down her cup and asked the waiter if she might have something to eat, some bread maybe? She wondered if she could have a glass of water.

Natalie ate and tried to set herself right, using her hand and elbow to hold up her head. She looked out the front of the restaurant, past the red booths and yellow lights and at the darkness settling on the Boulevard Saint-Germain. She marveled at how quiet it was outside.

Natalie was certain that Cecile from *Tristesse* would sleep with Donald. She would seduce him and leave him with the impression that it had been his idea from the start. Who knows, in this case maybe it had been. Donald had approached her after all.

Natalie put her hand down on her paperback and it was improving a bit, drying out on the table, but she knew it was going to be swollen like that forever.

Donald pulled a map of Paris from his jacket pocket and showed it to Natalie. The map was cut to pieces, rearranged and glued down on top of another map, an older map of Paris. Donald had been inspired by Debord and had been working on psychogeography for the last decade. After they'd kicked him out of the group he kept working. He told her that the police barricades around the Latin Quarter were facing bombardment. He wanted to watch as the city, the existing architecture, was transformed.

"You've got it all planned out?"

"Not at all," Donald said, but then he looked at his watch and asked if she wanted to enjoy a drink at the other café before they had to leave the Latin Quarter.

"Why do we have to leave?"

"Shall we go? You ready for more gin?"

At Les Deux Magots the gin was sweetened with soda, and the waiter refused to provide her with a porcelain mug but brought her a glass with ice, soda, and gin. Looking around it was otherwise much the same, more Greco-Roman columns, yellow electric lights, and booths with red leather upholstery.

Natalie unfolded Donald's collage of Paris. This Paris on an older map was smaller than the modern Paris that had been disassembled. The older map was denser. Natalie wondered if there might be dragons in the city.

"What year was the original map published?" she asked.

"1871." Donald downed another glass of wine all at one go.

"Do you think that this is a revolution? Do you think the situation will grow?" Natalie asked Donald.

"It doesn't matter what I think," he said. "It's up to the students, people in the factories, and beautiful young women in borrowed evening gowns."

The statues of the two Chinese merchants in straw bamboo hats for which the café was named looked down on Natalie and the rest of the tourists in the café with permanent condescending smiles. Natalie finished off her soda pop and gin and wiped her mouth with the back of her hand. "I'm tired of waiting for Sartre and Simone to show up here," she said.

"You don't like it here?" Donald asked.

"I remember now why Debord found his own café. Café Deux Magot. Besides, I'm not like Anna Karenina who has to wait for her big break."

Donald looked at his watch, and then shook his head. "We have another half-hour, are you sure?"

Boulevard Saint-Germain was lined with shop windows offering mannequins and posters of rock stars, antique commodities, and upscale disposables. They turned on Rue du Bac and crossed on Pont Royal. Donald took Natalie's hand as they stopped to look into the water. He let go right away though, to light a cigarette, and Natalie felt a pang of disappointment. Donald didn't really want to sleep with her, but really was only including her in his preconceived aesthetic moment. She wondered if Donald's being older was the source of his indifference. Walking together in silence, they reached the Louvre, the garden and the grandeur that had been the monarchy's but was currently the property of the people. There, as they wandered between palaces and enjoyed the fountains, she thought the best approach would be to be brazen.

"Why don't you want to sleep with me?" she asked.

"We've just met," Berreby said. "I'm a slow starter."

"We've met before."

"Did you hear about the French couple who set the world record?" Donald asked.

"No."

"They beat the Americans for how quickly one could visit the art. They sprinted through the museum in just over nine minutes. I believe they were newlyweds. I heard them interviewed on the radio. The girl seemed quite irritated by the whole scenario, but she'd participated so she had to answer the questions."

"That's about how long I'd want to stay inside. Art should be here, on the street."

Something caught Donald's eye and he walked away from her, toward the Palais Royal. Natalie stumbled a bit as she hurried to catch up. She was surprised when she entered the courtyard and saw what had diverted him. The courtyard was paved over in asphalt and divided up by painted dotted lines. Each plot of space, each rectangle, contained a short white concrete pillar with uniform black stripes running vertically around the base.

"What is this?" Natalie said.

The columns were striped like an awning from a bakery might be striped. They were simple, minimal, modern. Donald took her by her arm and led her onto the chessboard. Natalie imagined how they looked together arm in arm, a couple of beautiful people with licorice patterned novelties at their feet.

Natalie opened *Bonjour Tristesse* and found more lines about long caresses, passionate kisses, and bruised lips, but nothing about chessboards or licorice.

It began to rain, to mist, and Donald took off his overcoat and put it over Natalie's bare shoulders.

"You're lovely," he told her.

"I think I'm drunk," Natalie said. "Do you want to try to find us?" she asked him.

"What?"

Natalie held up the map of Paris that Donald had given her, spread it out on top of one of the taller columns.

"We could try to find ourselves on this map," she said. "Try to figure out where we are?"

"I don't think we're anywhere," Donald said. "We're off the map."

Natalie found Rue de Rivoli on the map, but it stopped before the Louvre. There was a cut.

Donald leaned over and pointed to all the places where he had drawn a circle, a blot. He ran his index finger along the lines connecting parts of the city to other parts, noted where they overlapped.

"That's the frame," he said.

"Do you ever test reality? Do you ever try to hold your breath or remember your childhood to make sure that what you think is real is actually real, actually true?" Natalie asked. She put her arms around his neck and her cheek against his. He had broad shoulders; his body felt hard but maybe a little thin against hers, and he was moving away from her.

"Damn," Natalie said. She opened *Tristesse* again, looked at page twenty-three and reread her favorite passage to herself instead.

"I think it's going to start," Berreby said.

"Wait, if we're outside the frame how do we hope to accomplish anything?" Natalie asked.

By the time the barricades went up Berreby had already said his goodbyes. It was still relatively early, but he had an appointment in another room with limestone walls, high ceilings, and champagne on ice.

Natalie, though, had to stay. She wandered the Latin Quarter in her high heels, still wearing Karen Wright's red evening gown, and watched as students from the Sorbonne unearthed cobblestones.

Christopher and Gerrard were released at nine pm. A lot had been happening while they'd been trapped under the police museum. Tens of thousands had taken to the streets demanding the release of all the prisoners from the May 3 protest, but this only made things more difficult for them as the police couldn't be seen to back down. When they did start releasing the students, first the boys and girls who were from good families (Natalie's dorm neighbor was among the first to go), they did so in secret. The police would come for a student in the middle of the night and lead him or her away from the cell block.

When they came for Christopher, when the guard told him that a mild British gentleman didn't belong in jail with ultra-leftist brats, Christopher objected.

If they were going to let Christopher go they had to release Gerrard at the same time. Christopher said that Gerrard was mentally ill, and that it was Christopher's job to look after him. Gerrard couldn't take care of himself, and would surely not survive in jail on his own.

The police, it turned out, were more than pleased to be rid of both of them. Christopher had merely confirmed a conclusion they'd reached on their own.

Opening brown envelopes by the prison gate Chris found his pocket watch was broken and his wallet empty, but he hadn't been robbed. His francs were in a separate plastic bag with a strange zipper along the top.

Gerrard took a pack of cigarettes out of his envelope and held it up to the light. Natalie had given him the packet nearly two months earlier during the March 22 occupation at Nanterre. Gerrard opened the packet, slipped out a cigarette, and then offered it to Chris who nodded and took it. Christopher said he didn't smoke. He'd tried to take up the habit during the war, but it hadn't worked out. Still, he accepted the cigarette, leaned in when Gerrard struck a match, and then let out coughs and gasps.

"Terrible," Chris said.

Gerrard took the cigarette from Chris, tried a puff himself. It was stale. He dropped the thing and stamped on it, and then put the packet back in the envelope.

As they approached Rue des Écoles, Gerrard recognized Natalie from behind. He recognized her shoulders and neck, her short blond hair, the way she held herself, the angle she made with her arms as she let her hands dangle below her hips. She was wearing a red dress held up by thin shoulder straps and stood facing Rue Saint-Jacques to the west. A crowd of students passed in front of her through the intersection, running from something.

Gerrard came up close to her, looked at the hair on the back of her neck, and Christopher walked to the opposite side of the street to find out what was happening. Gerrard put his hand on Natalie's bare shoulder and when she turned to see who it was he offered up his envelope, tipped it so that the packet of Gitanes fell into his open hand.

Natalie didn't seem pleased to see him at first; she didn't smile and she kept her arms folded defensively, but then she put her hands on her hips and accepted a cigarette when Gerrard tapped one out for her. Finally she made eye contact when she leaned forward and put the tip of her cigarette into the flame from the match Gerrard was holding.

"I've been thinking about you," Gerrard said.

"I heard you were arrested," she said.

"We just got out, actually."

"We?"

When Gerrard turned to introduce her to Christopher Robin Milne he found that the older man was gone. Chris was trying to cross Rue Saint-Jacques, but was instead being swept along with the crowd toward the Sorbonne. Impetuously Gerrard went after him. He took Natalie by the hand and dragged her with him into the crowd, but when they reached the intersection of Saint-Germain and Rue Saint-Jacques the crowd folded back on itself. People were pressed in shoulder-to-shoulder as everyone was trying to turn around as they came up against a police barricade at Rue des Écoles.

"We should stay together," Gerrard said.

Standing on the edge of Rue Saint-Jacques, looking over the heads of the students at Haussmann-style apartment buildings with wrought iron guardrails and neoclassical limestone façades, Gerrard realized he was standing in mud. The cream-colored limestone façades were set into soft earth, and the students had to work hard as they moved, step by step.

They caught up with Christopher Robin behind a pile of bricks. He was behind a student barricade on Boulevard Saint-Germain, pulling cobblestones up out of the mud and directing students on where to place each brick.

When Gerrard introduced Natalie to Christopher she offered her hand. She'd lost her shoes. She looked vulnerable standing in the mud between the upturned Renault convertibles and Peugeot sedans that formed a tricolor barrier. They were stooped behind a growing pile of bricks, behind the barricades, and she was shivering in her sleeveless red gown.

"Your skin is going to blister from the gas. You need a jacket, or better yet, to get out of here," Christopher said, and he offered her his trench coat. Natalie handed Gerrard her paperback as she put her arms in the sleeves.

Gerrard wandered away from them, stepping out from behind the barricade and onto the sidewalk exactly when the police launched the next round of tear gas grenades. The police were still at a distance as the green smoke spread across the cobblestones, but Gerrard couldn't move away fast enough in the mud.

The air was green and Gerrard was seeing dots, splotches. He moved his finger as if to connect the dots. He doubled over coughing, and that started him gagging and then vomiting.

It was Christopher who rescued him. He ran out into the street, caught Gerrard around the collar, and dragged him back behind the barricade.

The police arrived in their leather rain slickers and kepis, with their nightsticks and more tear gas grenades. They came down the street in formation, running in a line and shouting in unison, but as impressive as they were they had to stop. A hail of cobblestones greeted them and they fell back a meter, and then set up a grenade launcher. They let fly their grenades, again and again, and one of the students, a boy wearing glasses with black plastic frames and a neat button-up dress shirt, fell with his hands over his head. Gerrard couldn't tell what, if anything, had hit him, but he could see blood running down the boy's face. The police had hurt one of them.

They heard the police coming. They were yelling instructions, telling the students to disperse, and Natalie grabbed a paving stone. The two of them, Gerrard and Natalie, stood up so that they could see over the pile of bricks and past the overturned automobiles. A young man whose blond hair was just visible under his police helmet was very close, and Natalie took aim and moved her arm. The brick hit the young cop in the face. Gerrard heard the boy's nose break, and watched his blood spew out.

"That was very satisfying," Natalie said.

Someone handed Natalie a wet green towel for her to breathe through. She was still shivering even under Christopher's trench coat, but she didn't let her shivering stop her as she threw another cobblestone. The two of them heaved one stone after another, and Gerrard's arm grew tired, but he went on throwing. Something was moving through him, through them both.

19

W hen the desk clerk appeared, bleary-eyed but able to work, Christopher asked him if there was a shoe store nearby as he'd lost a loafer in the mud around the Sorbonne. Then he paid with a traveler's check and took a key for a room on the fifth floor. Gerrard had been right that the hotel was inexpensive, but there was little else that recommended it.

Christopher decided to get a drink at the bar before he went to his room. He didn't have to worry about his luggage because he'd lost his bags when he'd been arrested.

Chris ordered a Scotch whiskey, received it in a crystal tumbler, and listened to the conversation at the next table.

Three bellhops were sharing fantasies about a woman on the third floor—describing how they could take turns making it with her. She was apparently asking every man on the staff for his services.

"She's like Brigitte Bardot on a bicycle," said one.

"How's that?" asked one of the others.

"Liberated. The strike is blowing wind in her hair," replied the first one.

"But she's the one blowing." The third bellhop got a laugh.

Chris assumed they were on strike. He wondered why they'd come in at all. Shouldn't they have hit the streets rather than turning up at the hotel to play chess and smoke one cigarette after another? Christopher didn't understand what was motivating them, but sitting at the bar, watching them, he understood even less his own motivation.

Paris wasn't right for him. He wasn't a radical. He wanted none of the intrigue and nothing to do with the theories and fantasies of bellhops or college students. He'd been to a single socialist meeting in his life and that had been at Cambridge. A friend of his roommate's, a rather portly student who distinguished himself from the others by wearing a beard and, like Chris's father, smoking a cherry wood pipe, had asked if Christopher understood what socialism was all about. Christopher had admitted that he did not. He was not exactly sure of the definitions and facts involved.

"Why not find out? Come to a meeting. Discover it for yourself." The roommate's friend, perhaps his name had been John, had unfolded his arms in a gesture of expansive welcome.

The Cambridge socialists had quite nearly put Christopher off equality, fraternity, and liberty for good. They met in a pub near Cambridge called the Hogshead where they could drink lager and tea and proclaim absurdities.

The war in Europe was an imperialist war fought by competing imperialist powers and as an imperialist country England was fighting for British imperialism and nothing more. Real hope for the world revolution lay in India. Socialists would put it over big in India.

Chris had asked if, after the revolution, there would still be teatime. He hadn't liked the idea of putting things over, and especially hadn't liked the notion of putting whatever it was over big.

Even now Christopher felt he didn't fit into revolution. He was conventional, and it seemed to him that no revolution would abide him. No revolution could abide a man with a bookshop and a wife. And no revolution could really compete with the pleasure to be found on a garden path.

Christopher took a swig of whiskey and in a short while he was drunk.

Christopher even enjoyed the irrational aspects of owning a bookstore, the tricks and trade-offs. Even the fact that he had to sell trashy books in order to make a living seemed like the best thing to him. Selling such rot insured that he wouldn't become too pretentious or literary.

To be less than pure is what it meant to be grown-up. How had he allowed himself to be drawn into this childish dream? He'd fought the police on the streets as if he had something to prove. Did he want action, a battle?

He was still a bit drunk when he called Abby from a payphone in the hotel lobby. She was glad to hear his voice and wanted to know what had happened. He told her that he'd been in jail and tried to explain that he'd attacked a police officer and why, but he found that if he really wanted her to know about it he had to talk about the war instead.

Christopher had dropped out of Cambridge to join the army after seeing how London had suffered under German bombardment. The city seemed a long way off, but seeing the destruction, the ruined office buildings and walk-up flats, in the newspaper forced Christopher to confront the reality of what was happening. He'd had to do something to protect his home after seeing the photographs. He and his father set up booby traps and road-blocks along the road to Cotchford Farm.

The Germans never arrived there, the booby traps had been pointless, but even so it had been right to act. For while if the Germans had managed to take the Sussex coast they would have surely swept past his barbed wire and "dragon teeth" without any bother, the useless gesture had helped Christopher develop a willingness to resist. As absurd as his booby traps had been, they were part of a necessary first step.

After he talked to Abby he stopped worrying about the demonstrations, the police, and the boy who had brought him here, and let himself enjoy the tidiness of his hotel room and his view of the Parisian streets. He lifted the heavy frame windowpane, took a breath of air, and smelled the tear gas blowing along the boulevard.

Natalie brought Christopher his loafer around midnight. She knocked on the door to his room, handed him the shoe when he opened the door hotel room, and then let herself in and climbed onto the windowsill. She stood with her head against the ceiling. She had a bottle of gin in one hand and her copy of Sagan's book in the other.

She didn't know exactly what she wanted. On page seven of Sagan's novel Cecile admitted that she usually preferred her father's friends to the boys her age. The men of forty would speak to Cecile courteously and tenderly.

Natalie wondered if Christopher was looking at her legs. She stretched and turned her attention outward, through the window.

Paris was dark. She could see street lamps, dots of light, but the buildings and cars, the face of Paris, was occluded.

She stood up in the window and then walked along the edge of the room, fitting her bare feet on the molding. She climbed up into Christopher's closet, pulled herself onto a shelf above the wire clothes hangers, sat down, and then turned to look at him from above.

"Do you want a drink?" she asked.

"I'll have to get a cup," Christopher said.

Gerrard had asked her to fetch Christopher for him, to bring back the man who was famous for having once been a child. Gerrard thought he could help start a new story or dream, but Natalie was still trying to act out the second line on page seventy-one of *Bonjour Tristesse*:

> *For the first time in my life I had known the intense pleasure of analyzing another person, manipulating that person toward my own ends. It was a new experience. . . .*

She wanted to figure out Christopher for herself. She was climbing around his hotel room in order to discover the boundaries around him.

Christopher handed her a paper cup that he'd found by the sink and then handed Natalie an ashtray.

"Gerrard says you can help change things," she said.

"What things?"

Natalie watched Christopher Robin's eyes, and then pulled the hem of her red gown up just a bit so she could cross her legs.

"Do you believe in destiny?"

"No," Christopher said.

"Do you believe in cause and effect?"

"That's not really a matter of belief."

"How can you say you don't believe in destiny if you believe in cause and effect?" she asked.

Natalie took a sip of gin. Christopher's noble heritage, the values of Cambridge and the Queen, these things were right on the surface. He was wearing plastic rectangular glasses and an argyle sweater vest. Everything about the way he dressed and presented himself, even the way he sat there on the edge of the bed, communicated his class.

"Another splash of gin?" he asked.

"By all means," she said.

When she tried to catch his gaze with her own Christopher averted his eyes. He looked into her cup while he poured. When it was full she just kept holding it out toward him until he finally gave in and looked at her.

He smiled at her and she smiled back.

"Can I ask you a question?" she asked.

"Perhaps."

"What's a Heffalump?"

Christopher sighed. He stood up from the bed and walked to the window and for a moment she thought he was going to climb up next to her on the shelf, but he didn't. He stood there looking out.

"Your friend Gerrard is an unbalanced person," Christopher said.

"You think so?"

Christopher nodded but didn't look away from the glass.

"Then why are you here?" she asked.

His hotel room was very clean, cleaner than she would have expected, and yet it was still squalid. It was a tiny room with a high ceiling in a building that was three hundred years old.

There wasn't any dust. The walls were yellow from age, the paint was cracked, but everything was arranged properly.

"Did you tidy up your room?"

"What's that?"

"Did you dust?"

"I thought it would help me sleep. I didn't know you were coming, of course."

Natalie jumped down from her perch, refilled her cup with gin, and sat down on the edge of the bed. She patted the spot next to her, indicating Chris should come sit with her, but he just looked at her quizzically.

"Why did you turn up here again?"

"Gerrard asked me to deliver your shoe."

"Where is he then?" Christopher asked.

"We've occupied the Sorbonne."

"I see."

Christopher approached her, sat down next to her on the bed, and then stood up again. He went to the bedside table and unscrewed the top on the gin bottle, but hesitated there. He stood by the bed considering whether to refill his cup.

Natalie crossed her arms and waited. She wondered if she was making headway. Any number of girls could do what she was doing. Was that what free love was about, being anonymous? Her name was Natalie, but she might as well be named Cecile or Elsa or anything.

"You didn't answer me before," she said.

"What was the question?"

"What is a Heffalump?"

"Have you read my father's books?" he asked.

She hadn't but Gerrard had told her a few of the stories. He'd told her about the toy animals and the forest. He'd told her about how Christopher Robin promised his bear to always remember.

"A Heffalump is an imaginary elephant," Chris said. He poured himself the drink and sat down next to her.

"An elephant?"

"An imaginary elephant. It's the kind of creature that if one sets a trap for it one will only catch one's self."

Natalie leaned back on her elbows and closed her eyes for a moment. "Gerrard says that we're looking for Heffalumps."

"That's a damning assessment," Christopher said perfunctorily.

"Gerrard doesn't think so," she said.

She reached out to Christopher and grabbed the back of his neck. He fell on her then, but not too clumsily. She put her tongue in his mouth. He tasted of coffee and spearmint gum. They rolled together on the bed, mussing the sheets, and she ended up on top of him, straddling his waist.

Christopher's spectacles were askew. He took them off.

"Do you believe in God, Natalie?"

"No." Maybe her parents had believed in God, but she didn't believe. To her God was the smiling man on a billboard at the Metro station, or in a magazine. He was a new bra, a canned soup, or a wrapped stick of licorice. Natalie was no longer the good Catholic girl who prayed to Jesus and licorice. Natalie wanted to be an ingrate. She wanted to reject God and the society He spoke through.

"I don't believe either, not in God or Heffalumps," he said. He lifted Natalie off, set her to the side, and then sat up and turned to get out of bed. "You have to be going now."

"I do?"

Christopher took Natalie's pack of cigarettes from the shelf above the closet and took the bottle of gin from the nightstand. He held these out to her.

Natalie took the bottle from him, but had Chris tap out the last cigarette for her on the spot.

She breathed in the smoke and let it out.

"What is it that you want?" she asked.

"I don't want anything."

"Then what are you doing here? Why are you in Paris?"

Christopher didn't answer, but opened the door. She took another puff of her cigarette and waited for an answer.

"Goodbye."

She walked where he pointed, and it was only when she passed through, only once she was out in the hallway, that she remembered Gerrard.

"Wait. You're supposed to come with me," she said.

20

That morning, inside the art studio at the National School of the Fine Arts, Christopher joined the propaganda committee. The room was bordered by poster boards hanging off clotheslines. There were a half-dozen worktables, each with a plastic tub full of dyes and other chemicals, a clay cup filled with pens and scalpels, and a wooden silk-screen frame. A girl wearing round glasses and a denim work shirt with the sleeves rolled up, whose long brown hair was pulled up into a bun, took a rolling pin and pressed ink through taut silk. She used a putty knife to separate the paper from the frame.

The silk-screened monochromatic posters were colored red or black or blue or green, and Christopher felt strangely optimistic looking at them. The cartoon of a blue policeman wearing a helmet and goggles and brandishing a club behind a shield printed on cream-colored paper was somehow familiar.

"I have a poster like this, in this style, at home," he said. "Found it in my shop back in 1961."

"One of these?" Gerrard asked. "Which one?"

One featured a graphic that combined the Sorbonne Chapel with the iconography of a factory. The poster's simple affirmation was "Popular University? Yes!" Another depicted Prime Minister Georges Pompidou as a chicken. Another featured an iconic factory along with the words "May 68, the beginning of a prolonged fight."

"They're all of a piece," Christopher said. "They all have same graphic style, but none of these are exactly the one."

There was a set of agreed-upon symbols, a particular aesthetic, that one had to adopt in order to join the committee, but once you learned the rules it was easy to participate. Natalie showed him a poster she'd designed. A hand smashed through the poster itself, a raised fist broke the medium, and the slogan was "Break through your life."

Another poster depicted a woman with her head wrapped in bandages and with a safety pin holding her mouth closed. Her eyes were shaped targets. The caption read "A youth disturbed too often by the future."

Christopher found his poster after Gerrard cut the paper into a stencil of a brown bear sitting with a honey pot in the middle of a circle of riot police. The bear bared its teeth as the police cowered behind their batons ineffectively. There were two figures with the bear. One was embracing the bear, standing on its lap and hugging the beast around the neck, while the other was kneeling to the bear's left. The slogan written above the frame read:

VOUS NE RÉCUPÉREREZ PAS CET OURS DANS SON CAGE.

Gerrard made the poster with orange paint and yellow paper and a silk screen. He pressed out three hundred copies.

That afternoon the three of them joined a contingent of students from the occupied Sorbonne, mostly March 22 organizers and other members of Les Enragés, in a march to the Renault factory. Gerrard and Natalie carried bundles of posters and Christopher carried the red enamel stockpot full of wheat paste.

The other students were in dress clothes—black sports jackets and skinny ties on the men, khaki skirts and black turtleneck sweaters on the women—but Gerrard and Natalie were unwashed and ragged. Gerrard was still in the same American blue jeans he'd been wearing since Christopher met him in jail and Natalie in a no-longer-elegant evening gown. She was wearing a pair of saddle shoes instead of high heels but while these had flat soles they didn't really fit her. Natalie's shoes kept slipping off her feet as she walked.

Christopher's own loafers were still damp from having been washed in the sink in his hotel room, and as the cobblestones gave way to cement and then to mud as the streets widened he could feel water seep through the leather and into his socks.

A crowd of autoworkers milled around outside the gates as a union representative in a three-piece wool suit stood on a platform to the right and sweated through his clothes. He spoke slowly into a microphone and informed everyone that this was a one-day strike; they were occupying the factory and if the workers who were waiting outside would join their comrades inside they'd find a general assembly in progress.

Natalie nudged Christopher and pointed to the roof of the factory where about a hundred workers in overalls and caps were standing. They waved down to the pale, bespectacled students. When they had the students' attention they pressed in together at the roof's edge. For a moment Gerrard thought that they were going to jump, but rather than self-destruct the workers began to sing. Christopher recognized the tune.

It was "The Internationale," and most of Les Enragés and the March 22 group sang back without hesitation.

"We should get to work," Gerrard said. He pointed toward the double doors and then changed his mind and pointed to the left of these.

Christopher worried that the posters wouldn't stick to the rough brick surface of the factory wall, but he followed him into the crowd and they used wide paintbrushes to apply wheat paste to the wall, filling the cracks with the snot-colored gel. They spread out a poster depicting Charles de Gaulle's silhouette as the spokes inside multiple gears, ran their hands over the poster to push the air bubbles to the edges. De Gaulle's nose was what made him identifiable; it jutted out well past the length of the brim of his kepi cap.

The slogan at the bottom of the poster read: "Let us break the old gears."

The next poster also featured gears, only these were line drawings, circles without teeth. A hand emerging from the right side of the page was shown to stop the turning of the mechanism by sticking a finger between the gears, and the slogan read: "To yield just a little is to capitulate much."

As they worked they sang, "So comrades, come rally, and the last fight let us face. The international working class shall be the human race."

When the song was finished the speaker for the Confédération Général du Travail stepped forward again but just stammered into the microphone. The problem of the milling workers who shuffled back and forth outside the factory became more obvious. They were immigrants and spoke Italian or Algerian Arabic, and they weren't following the instructions he'd given them in French. The man covered the microphone with his right hand and leaned back to listen to another union official who had joined him on the platform. This second bureaucrat was thinner, seemed more comfortable in his blue suit, and he whispered instructions as the first man nodded. The first bureaucrat straightened his blue vest, wiped away the sweat from his brow, and pushed his stringy black hair back into place over his bald spot.

"I understand that the students from the Sorbonne would like to be of some use, and that there is a standing offer to translate the message of the strike for the foreign workers." The bureaucrat leaned back again to his superior officer. "The CGT would like to accept that offer. And we'd ask that any of the students who speak Arabic or Italian approach the stage."

They were pasting up the first Pooh poster when Natalie handed Christopher her bundle and stepped back into the crowd. Natalie walked up to the platform, stepped onto the wooden stage, and crossed over to the CGT official. When the bureaucrat handed Natalie the pages of text he'd been reading from and he pointed to where he wanted her to begin, she stepped forward, squinting against the sun, and cleared her throat.

She spoke Italian, not quite fluently, but well enough, probably better than Chris did. She read, " 'The workers of the Renault factory have occupied the factory. The CGT called a strike on the thirteenth in solidarity with those who had been arrested and against the mischief of the police, and today the workers have chosen to continue the strike not only out of solidarity, but out of self-interest. We have our own demands.' "

Christopher wondered how it could be that he had a duplicate of the orange or brownish poster that he'd helped bring to
the factory stored in a cardboard box at home. What could the
anomaly possibly mean? There was not, as far as he could tell,
any mundane explanation for it, but if it was some kind of super-
natural event it was one of those inscrutable miracles that in
Sunday school had always seemed absurd to him. What use
could the poster have been back in 1961, and what use was the
strangeness of it now that he was in the right context for the message?

"'We are forced to live in prefabricated rooms that are ugly
and unsanitary, and we denounce the bunk beds stacked to the
ceiling,'" Natalie read in her halting Italian. "'The working
man can't sit up in the morning but must lie flat on the hard flat
mattress provided by management. Even when we are out of bed
there is nowhere to sit. In each room there are only six chairs for
twelve men, and we take turns sitting down.

"'We have no health centre. There is no first aid available.
When we are sick we have to pay for our own treatment and stay
in these small rooms, spreading our illness to our comrades.'"

Natalie glanced ahead on the list, flipped ahead in the pages,
reading out loud, translating bits and pieces as she went.

"'There is a total lack of entertainment, except for one TV
set,'" she muttered. "'All visits, including those by families, are
forbidden. Taking photographs is forbidden. Newspapers, leaflets,'" Natalie translated. And then she looked up and spoke
without the script. "Only none of this is true. Not anymore.
Your comrades have taken the factory. Look and see," she said.
"None of these old rules apply. You don't need to make these
demands of the owners. The factory belongs to you now."

Natalie dropped the notes on the podium, and then changed

her mind and picked the pages up and threw them into the crowd. The bureaucrat rushed over to her and nudged her out the way. He said, in French, "These students are trying to arouse division in our ranks and weaken us."

Natalie pushed back and shouted into the microphone. "The students support you." Natalie said it in French, and then in Italian, and then in French again. "We've taken our university, and now that we have it, it is yours as well," she said. "What is the union promising? A vacation? A color TV?" she asked.

When the CGT official took a swing at her Natalie backed off the platform. She walked away from the microphone and toward the factory gates, toward the double doors, and Gerrard pulled Christopher away from the Pooh poster so they could catch her before she went in.

They marched together to the entrance, to the factory doors, just the three of them, while the other students hung back with the foreign workers, talking to them, passing out leaflets.

Gerrard pulled on the latch; the doors were locked. The CGT had locked them out of the factory and no matter how hard Gerrard pulled, the doors didn't budge.

21

G errard led Christopher down the narrow streets of Paris
and as they walked along he examined the cracked mud
that had replaced the cobblestones. It turned out that underneath the cobblestones there was mud instead of a beach. Gerrard had been hoping to find a forest with trees hundreds of feet
tall, a forest to get lost in, but there was only mud, and the streets
were still littered with the cobblestones that had been torn up,
bricks that had been knocked down, and autos turned sideways.

Two women in wool dresses and knit jackets helped each other
climb the remnants of barricades that blocked both the street and
sidewalk on Rue Dante. They linked arms, held their shopping
bags between them as ballast, and gingerly stepped up the pile of
loose bricks.

"Yes! Factories Occupied." The sign to Gerrard's left was
stuck to a lamppost with wheat paste and cohered to the ridges
in the lamp's base. The paste had seeped through the paper so
that the red text on the poster had turned purple.

Gerrard had not slept in four days. He wanted to test out

what was possible without it, what would happen if he continued to experience elements of dreaming while he was awake.
How long could a waking dream be maintained?

"You need to invent a new game," Gerrard told Christopher.
"The same new game your father made up."

"How do you mean?"

The idea was that by derailing Christopher Robin he might
be able to find the Hundred Acre Wood, the dreamtime, that lay
obscured under layers of stone and soot. Bringing Christopher
Robin into the strike was Gerrard's attempt to reuse his story as
material for another dream, a new dream lived out at a higher
level. Gerrard continued toward the river, counting his steps
and breathing in the green air, and he tried to explain it to him.

"All the usual ways that we go about living our lives, the routines and reasons given, can no longer get a purchase on reality.
We're losing our grip," he said.

"You're losing your grip?" Christopher asked. "It seems like
you've let go."

They reached a small bookstore on Rue de la Bûcherie and
stopped where shards of glass from the broken storefront, tat-
tered paperbacks and shelving lay strewn across the hard mud.
Christopher stopped and bent down to look at the titles.

"How can I look at this and think anything good about this
strike and its aims?" he asked. "Where is the hope in this kind
of thing?"

Gerrard picked through the books in order to see if there
might be anything good to read among the loot. They were all
in English, or were English translations, and only a few of the
names on the book jackets were familiar to him (Coelho, Ca-
mus, Clausewitz) while most were unknown. The majority of
the books left behind appeared to be fantasies or science fiction

by Britons and Americans. They had green, purple, and black covers with names like Lafferty, Russ, and Silverberg underneath the titles.

Gerrard picked up one, a book titled *The Time Hoppers* that depicted a businessman with a briefcase with a rainbow emerging from his fedora. Green and blue arrows pointed back into the darkness. Gerrard turned the book over and read the blurb on the back: "A brilliant new novel about a future so suffocating that the only way to escape from a totally controlled environment is to 'hop' backward through time."

Gerrard put the book in the back pocket of his trousers, and then looked down at the other titles to make sure there was nothing that he'd missed.

"You taking that?" Christopher asked.

"Or I could leave it in the mud?"

Gerrard picked through them, flipped each book over to read the back cover, but didn't find anything else to his liking and was about to move on when he noticed something in the display case in the store window. A red-and-black wooden yo-yo was dangling out of the broken window. Gerrard fished it out from the shards of glass. He looped the string around his middle finger, tossed the toy toward the cobblestones, and was delighted to discover that the device returned to his hand before it hit the ground. Up and down.

Christopher frowned but didn't object again.

On Quai de la Tournelle, Gerrard tossed his yo-yo toward the water, and it spun over the river before snapping back to his hand. He tossed it again toward his feet and the yo-yo went down the string, touched down on the mud, and stuck there. The line was taut. The yo-yo was caught in the soft, shifting ground of Paris.

"You need to invent a new game," Gerrard said again.

But Christopher just shrugged. He'd never invented any games. Gerrard was misremembering. Christopher Robin, the character, was the straight man for the animals and if Gerrard wanted him to start adventures or make up rhymes then he wanted him to act outside of his character.

"That was Winnie-the-Pooh," Christopher said. "That's why the game was called Pooh Sticks."

It had been the bear who'd stumbled onto the game of Pooh Sticks. The bear had tripped and dropped something into the river. He'd been surprised when whatever it was showed up on the other side of the bridge he'd been crossing. He'd dropped the thing on one side of the bridge but it turned up on the other side.

"Pinecones. He dropped pinecones," Christopher said.

Still, even if Christopher hadn't invented the game he knew how to play it. Maybe that would be good enough. They could try it out on the River Seine and see if the new game of dropping things over the side and waiting for them to reemerge would be good enough.

"You said that you wanted to take parts of my father's stories and put them into a new context?" Christopher asked. "Well, the story is that Edward Bear invented Pooh Sticks."

Before they could hash it out any further they were interrupted by a few police officers who were approaching from the east. There were four police officers with two boys, students, set between them. These men were separated into two groups of three and in each group the policemen walked on the right and left leaving the youngster in the middle.

Gerrard let out the string on his yo-yo, attempted to unspool it quickly, and found that there were many meters of thread twisted round and round the spindle. He could hear the police talking as they approached and could just make out the students as they argued back.

"You two aren't fun anymore," one of the students complained to the policeman on his left.

"I've outgrown fun," the first policeman said.

Gerrard pulled his yo-yo out of the soft mud and then tossed it so that the string looped around the pole of a street lamp that faced the water. The yo-yo continued to unwind and slip down, until it finally disappeared into the water, but Gerrard held the string and the two of them walked across to the other side of the road where Chris quickly tied the other end to a tree branch.

The other policeman was now talking. "It's not that we don't admire your ideas. It's not that they're bad ideas, if they could be acted on. But human nature just won't allow for it." He and his partner stepped forward and hit the string. They stopped and then each absently brought a hand to the forehead.

The other group of three men came up on this and again the two policemen were stopped at the string. They put their hands up, attempted to untangle themselves, while the students ducked. The second student, the thinner of the two, a man with brown hair and a suede jacket, stepped over to where his blond friend in the grey sweater was waiting.

"Everything is reduced to an abstraction. Everything is reducible to its economic representation and no longer has value in and of itself," he told one of the policemen who was twisting backward and flapping his hands up and down the front of his jacket.

"Wait a moment," the policeman said. "I'm still listening. I've just got something caught on a button."

The two students watched for a moment as the police swatted

the air and then realized their opportunity. They turned the corner at a full run. One policeman stood up straight and watched
them go, and then took off after them, breaking the yo-yo string
as he went. The rest of the men followed along after.

"Looks like you've invented the new game," Christopher
said.

Gerrard laughed and started to untie the yo-yo string from
the tree branch, but decided to leave it. He was tired, and
crossed over to the water again. He sat on the bank of the Seine,
dangled his feet over the water, and then lay back on the cobblestones and let his body relax, let himself sink a bit into the
ground.

With his eyes closed, he let his breathing slow, and he considered Natalie, the shape of her face, and the way her lips felt when
he kissed her, and wondered how it was that he'd lost her.

The phone was ringing. Gerrard was no longer lying on the
bank of the Seine, but was lying in the thick grass of the Jardin
du Luxembourg. And he could hear a phone ringing. His feet
were in dirt. He was kicking over large pink flowers. The camel-
lias were planted in the moist sod in perfect lines. On the other
side of the garden there was a large white tent, entirely common-
place and yet also perfectly extraordinary.

The phone rang again. It seemed to be coming from the tent.

Gerrard felt certain that he'd find elderly women in yellow
V-neck sweaters, and all manner of other upper-crust Gaullists
inside, all of them drinking champagne, but when Gerrard pulled
the tent flaps open and stepped inside he found the tent was
empty except for full-length mirrors, a red wooden table with a
green phone set atop it, and red-and-white-striped floorboards.

The mirrors created the impression that the tent was twice as wide as it actually was, and when Gerrard stepped up to the ringing phone he felt as if he was standing in the middle of a vast open room where he could be seen from all sides even though the table was right up against the glass.

"Hello?"

The woman's voice sounded familiar even though she wasn't speaking French or English, but like something that reminded Gerrard of American Westerns. The woman on the other end of the line sounded like Tonto from *The Lone Ranger*.

"Nyangurnangku," the woman said.

"Hello? Who is this?"

"You are not alone. I can see you," the woman said.

Gerrard looked back and forth, into the mirrors, at the space in between the stripes, but he didn't see anyone there in the tent with him. He put the phone back to his ear and started over.

"Hello?"

"There is a structure to the dreaming, Gerrard. It isn't your dreaming alone, isn't anyone's dreaming. The dreaming came first. Do you understand?"

"Hello?" Gerrard asked his greeting.

Somebody else came on the line. The voice was that of a child. The little boy recited in English, "When I was one I had just begun," he said. "When I was two I was still brand new."

Gerrard put down the phone and walked out of the tent and across the street to the Odeon Theatre. He did not stop to consider how far away the Odeon actually was from the Jardin du Luxembourg, or stop to think that he'd exited through the same door flaps that he'd entered and managed to end up somewhere different from where he'd begun.

Gerrard wanted to test the logic of the moment, to see and

understand the new cause and effect, but instead he walked up the steps of the Odeon Theatre, between the Greco-Roman columns, and to the large oak doors.

The theater had been taken by the students and was being used as a meeting hall. Opening the doors was a shock. He moved from silence to the din of a conversation among thousands. Five haggard-looking professors and students sat stoically in metal folding chairs on the stage while in the balconies above, the din of voices grew louder. A young man illuminated by a spotlight leaned over the railing on the third level. He ran his hand over his unruly beard and shouted so that spittle flew out of his mouth and presumably down onto the people sitting on the main floor below.

"This is not normal, and we cannot pretend that what is happening now can be sustained indefinitely. Eventually people will wake up, and the dream will end," the young man yelled.

"You mean the workers will eventually go back to sleep. They are awake now," one of the older men on stage said. He adjusted his glasses and spoke softly into the microphone in front of him.

Gerrard felt somebody's cold hand on his neck, and when he turned to look who it was he found Natalie standing next to him.

"Where have you been?" she asked him.

He didn't know how to answer.

22

G errard was inside the Sorbonne with hundreds of others, pressed against a window and looking out at the other two wings of the university's Cour d'Honneur. The student by the folding chairs at the front of the crowd held up a megaphone and denounced de Gaulle. He was an unshaven but otherwise tidy young man. Gerrard thought he recognized him from the Conterscarpe Café or maybe from the March 22 occupation. The young man explained the moment, denounced de Gaulle's own denunciation of the strike.

What de Gaulle had said was simple: "Reform yes, but no chaos." More precisely what he'd said was *"la reforme oui, la chienlit non."* A *chienlit* was a masquerade, a carnival or a chaos, but this word could be heard a different way. It could be heard as chie-en-lit or "shit in bed." He thought the president was speaking in code.

" 'He insinuates that we are children and that this movement is a movement of the bowels. He says that we are so out of control that we are shitting ourselves, but notice that to indict us he had to turn to an anachronism. He says we should reject the carnival mask, the masquerade, but is what we're doing a carnival or masquerade? Isn't it more the case that everyday life under de Gaulle, that this new technocracy is a masquerade? In fact, this economy or society is a spectacle that insists that we live under masks. We are to be dominated by the different roles available in the market.'" The young man was reading from a composition notebook with a red cover and the crowd was shifting on the wood floor in front of him. He read in a monotone and mechanically turned the pages in his notebook.

The student pointed out that in the seventeenth century Pascal put his finger on what was so obvious now. Three hundred years before the Office de Radiodiffusion-Télévision Française and programs like *Jeux Sans Frontieres,* Pascal saw how the games we play, or our daily masquerades, are killing us.

"'We would live according to the ideas of others,'" the student read. "'We would live an imaginary life, and to this end we cultivate appearances. Yet in striving to beautify and preserve this imaginary state of being we neglect everything authentic.'"

He told the crowd that if their usual lives were masquerades then the strikes and occupations were ways of stepping out of the usual carnivalesque dance and into reality. And that meant that the shit in the bed was de Gaulle himself and not the strike. Not the radical break.

Gerrard glanced out and spotted Natalie in the crowd in the courtyard. She'd found a change of clothes since Gerrard had seen her last and she looked quite beautiful in a black wool coat and a clean blouse. He couldn't tell for sure, but she might've been wearing lipstick.

"Hello, Cecile," he said when he caught up to her in the courtyard. "How is your search for free love going?"

She looked up at him and then returned to staring at the ground. She shuffled her feet in the mud and pursed her lips. "It's always a mess when you're around."

Gerrard felt confident that she'd missed him. He just needed to confront her with this fact and to let her know that his feelings hadn't changed. They could carry on. The occupation made cohabitation easy even if privacy was still a rare luxury. Besides, she needn't go on trying to realize Sagan's little best seller in the midst of a full-on revolution. She should put aside such a partial project, especially now.

"Free love is for the hippies. It's an American idea now, all about dressing like Indians and screwing pop stars outdoors, in the bushes in Central Park. If you want to realize that all you need do is follow the instructions you find in *Elle* or *L'Express*," Gerrard said.

"Where is your friend Christopher Robin?" Natalie asked.

Christopher Robin was pretending to be a tourist, mostly hanging around his hotel, but occasionally venturing out to catch the usual sights. He'd taken Christopher to see the Arc de Triomphe, for instance.

Natalie brushed her hair out of her eyes and finally looked at him, and he reached out and took her by the hand.

Natalie had a paper bag full of groceries with her, just some stale baguettes and hardened brie, but it tasted good to him. They found a spot under a poster of Chairman Mao to sit and discuss what they wanted to do next.

They were surrounded by feet clad in leather dress shoes and girls in respectable flats and hosiery. A shuffling crowd ebbed and flowed around them as they leaned on the limestone façade and rested against the ornate pillars around the door's transom. Natalie put her head on his shoulder as he laid out their options. He put down three books on the hard mud.

The first book was *The Time Hoppers*. Written by an American named Silverberg, the cover depicted cartoon arrows that pointed back on themselves canceling their own direction, a man with a rainbow instead of a head, and a melted stopwatch.

"It's about how a midlevel bureaucrat handles the possibility that a time traveler, or more a company of time travelers, might upset the delicate temporal structure, the chain of cause and effects, that supports the institutions of power that he is sworn to protect. The story goes along, each character is constrained by his or her own personal desires, and in the end nothing changes. Even time travel can't alter the teleological principle at work in the book or shift the way power acts and controls the characters."

Next Gerrard put down his own copy of *Bonjour Tristesse*. The illustration on the cover depicted the curved backside of a young woman, her bottom visible through a transparent dress. She was bracketed by blue and red rectangles. The tricolor held her in the centre white space.

"This one—"

"Let me," Natalie said. "It is, like the science fiction novel, about what's impossible. The protagonist, the young Cecile, is the most conservative character in the book. She clings to a routine and debauched life and is willing to destroy any and all threats to her lack of self-awareness. She wards off all introspection and in the end her only freedom is the freedom to say hello to her sadness," Natalie said.

He kissed her at that moment. She responded, even slipped her tongue in his mouth; when they paused, when the embrace loosened so as to let in air, she leaned away from him. She backed off.

"Gerrard. Don't. Please," she said.

The girl with black hair parted in the middle was from Nanterre. She read aloud from *L'Humanité* in the courtyard of the Sorbonne and a ring of other girls listened. Natalie recognized them but she couldn't remember any of their names.

They were getting the moment wrong anyhow. Each of them seemed to enjoy the newspaper description and miss the threat in it. The paper reported a split between the workers and students. The paper informed the reader that Daniel Cohn-Bendit was the leader of Les Détournés, but there was no split, and Cohn-Bendit wasn't with Les Détournés. Cohn-Bendit was some sort of independent anarchist. Natalie had heard rumors that he'd fallen out with Debord in public. The redheaded media darling had slapped Debord during a chance encounter at the École des Beaux-Arts.

Natalie did not know where the strike was headed and certainly did not feel confident enough to stand around giggling at their troubles. Instead she wandered off. She examined the walls that were light brown or a kind of yellow. The Sorbonne was very beautiful.

What Natalie wanted was some sort of intuitive sense of how the student strike, the factory occupations, and the strangeness that came along with both of these might succeed, but Debord didn't approve of Henri Bergson.

Bergson claimed that you had to go beyond rational thought in order to know anything, and this struck Debord as softheaded. Still, Natalie couldn't see any other way to get past the surface of the moment. All of them, the upper-crust but disenchanted students who felt at home with the Louis Treize architecture, the young workers in leather jackets who obviously were eager to help Natalie or any other girl find free love, and all the rest of the people on strike were playing a game of pretending, but they didn't have any end point in mind. The students around her in the courtyard were spinning around and around, all of them debating what should come next, but only settling on one simple idea.

They would continue the occupation.

The only way they might win was if Bergson was right. If rationality was not necessary, or if it was even a hindrance, then they could prevail. They could ride the moment for the full duration, just let it move them along. Spontaneous action would give them an intuitive grasp on the totality.

And Natalie had almost convinced herself when Gerrard turned up and what had seemed like a kind of foundation turned to mud.

Gerrard had his own theory about *Bonjour Tristesse*.

"The point of Sagan's book is that freedom requires more than just doing what you want with your body. It's not even about what you do with your mind. It's about choosing how you want to be constrained. Cecile wasn't manipulative enough— she thought she wanted to be free but what she wanted was to continue being trapped by the things she was accustomed to—"

The Sorbonne was pressing in on them and Natalie reached for Gerrard's broad shoulders. She could find comfort in his wild eyes and mussed hair.

She had some food for him and watched him chew for a time.

She could see something like love in his eyes, and she wanted to love him back. Maybe stale baguette and hardened brie would be enough.

They sat together under a poster of Chairman Mao and Gerrard asked her to help him choose what to derail next. Christopher Robin hadn't worked out quite the way he'd hoped and Gerrard was reconsidering. He had a science fiction novel, and a copy of Sagan's book.

"In Debord and Wolman's guide for derailing art they say the most distant element works best," she told him. She'd let herself lean on Gerrard, wasn't thinking about what she was doing or how he'd respond. "For instance, if you're collaging a photograph from the past you could combine it with something very current like an advertisement, and get a revolutionary effect. Debord describes a metagraph relating to the Spanish Civil War and says that the phrase with the most distinctly revolutionary sense is a fragment from a lipstick advertisement. The phrase, 'Pretty lips are red.'"

Gerrard tried to kiss her and she let him, but even as she arched her back she thought about Cecile in *Bonjour Tristesse*. What if it turned out that the words *free* and *love* were opposites? What if the freedom necessary for intuition required her to give up on love?

Gerrard was wild but his desire was predictable, and the romance he was offering her was routine. To be his girl, to be filled up with his love would mean betraying the uncertainty she'd found, and she couldn't afford to lose her uncertainty. It was the only kind of freedom she knew.

"Gerrard. Don't. Please."

23

Abby Milne arrived at the hotel on Rue du Four on the morning of May 20. She and Daniel paused at the entrance. Before she opened the door, before stepping from the cobblestone street into the cramped lobby, she glanced to the left at the apartment building built right up against the hotel, at the corner between the two buildings, and saw that she was being watched. A man was looking down at her from a small window, just large enough for the top half of his head to be visible. Realizing that she was being watched, making eye contact unexpectedly, she found that she couldn't bring herself to go in.

She stood on the doorstep, looked up and down the street, and then walked around the hotel to the right. She passed a much larger window, a window into the hotel bar and café where Christopher was looking for someone to serve him tea. Chris spotted his family as they passed but they didn't see him. Instead of stopping Abby turned the corner, stepped between beige walls on a tiny street, a space from an older Paris.

Standing there holding Daniel's hand with her right hand

and holding her green tweed suitcase with the other she took a deep breath and tried to consider. She and Daniel were both exhausted by the day's travel. That morning she'd had to chase him across the deck of the ferry and had nearly dropped him into the channel. She'd set him down on the railing in order to get him at eye level and he was such a skinny little boy, so small, that when she'd set his rear on the rail and he'd squirmed she'd been sure he was going overboard. She'd held tight to his sweater, pulled him back onto the deck, and then cursed herself for her stupidity. She'd wanted to stop his running, wanted to tell him how dangerous it was, and she'd set him on the rail?

After the incident she'd insisted they spend the rest of the journey in the enclosed passenger area. She'd parked herself in a plastic bucket seat and let Daniel run up and down the aisles, no longer caring if he was disturbing other passengers, but just glad he was relatively safe.

Abby stood in the alleyway, with her little blond son on her hip, and silently chastised herself. She imagined that she wasn't really in Paris yet. The train ride had been a blur and some part of her remained on the ferry, out on the Channel. When Christopher opened the employee exit in front of her, when he stepped out into the very narrow street with her, she was a bit bewildered.

"I told you not to come," Christopher said. "Who's minding the Harbour?"

She didn't say anything, but put Daniel down and watched him run to his father. Chris picked the boy up and slung him onto his shoulders.

"It's not safe to run," Daniel said. "Not safe to run."

Christopher bounced the boy on his shoulders and kissed his wife. "How was the journey? How are you?"

The water in the English Channel was cold, the early morning sky had been dark green, and she'd convinced herself that they'd never see Christopher again. On the ferry, crossing over, she'd been sure she'd lost him. Why did he insist that they wait before having a child? She didn't have the energy to raise the boy on her own.

"Christopher," she said. She was so glad to see him that she could hardly believe he was right there in front of her.

"Let's go inside," he said. He started to turn around to go through the same door he'd come through before, but Abby grabbed his hand and turned him back. She kissed him, and then looked around, tried to get her bearings.

"We made it. We're in Paris," she said.

The next morning Christopher and his family sat at a sidewalk table outside the hotel, picked up menus neatly placed between utensils, and prepared to order breakfast. Daniel sat in Abby's lap, moving his spoon back and forth across the cloth napkin that was folded on the iron mesh tabletop, making the spoon talk to the table knife, saying, "Free our comrades" and "Welcome to the Woodentops."

Christopher watched his son and wondered if he could turn what had been a disruption of his established life into a vacation instead, but as they waited for someone to appear to take their order, when ten minutes ticked by and then a half-hour, the reality of the situation reasserted itself. The CGT had joined with the student groups and called a one-day general strike. Nobody would be coming to wait on them.

Rue du Four was grey and cool. Christopher looked down at the cobblestones and his stomach grumbled. Daniel's monologue with the spoon seemed to be deteriorating.

"Stupid man. Stupid bad," the spoon said accusingly.

They would have to do something on their own about break-fast. He turned to Abby and shrugged, hoping she might have a better idea than his own, but as far as he could see they'd have to break into the café's kitchen.

"Let's just hope the pantry is still well stocked," Abby said.

Luckily someone, probably one of the younger cooks or wait-ers, had left the kitchen unlocked and even gone so far as to leave a note on the door welcoming the hotel's guests and suggesting they make themselves an omelet. The guests were asked to limit their consumption to one egg each. It was, the note explained, important to conserve resources during the strike. Abiding by the one-egg-for-each rule and limiting the consumption of cream was requested as a show of solidarity.

Christopher grated cheese into the pan and had layered his disc of a crepe when Gerrard opened the door to the kitchen and shouted in triumph, "Here you are!"

Gerrard stood in the doorway and watched the Milne family cook breakfast. He joined them out on the sidewalk and at Abby's urging ate two crêpes. Christopher sat silent, pushing the pieces of his crêpe back and forth, and eyeing Gerrard.

"We're going to the zoo today," Gerrard said.

"Are we?"

Abby concentrated on her cup of espresso, raising it to her lips and taking sips, and Daniel used his fork and spoon to act out another small drama. The utensils were lonely, their papa had left them, and their mother was a butter knife on the moon.

"We're going to try again," Gerrard told him. "You were right before. You can't invent a new game on your own. You need your bear if you're going to do anything."

"We're going to the zoo to find a bear?" Chris asked.

"That's right. And we've got to get going," he said. Gerrard stood up.

"Wait a moment," Christopher said. "Let's clear the table first."

"Good idea," Abby said.

"Equality. Fraternity. Dishes." Christopher took his wife's empty plate away.

On the way to the Paris Zoo, Gerrard told them what was happening. According to newspapers nearly ten million people were on strike, not only in Paris but throughout the rest of France as well. Gerrard told him that the cross channel ferries were on duty, but the railroad and Metro workers were out. The department stores were closed; the nation's television personalities were off the air. According to Gerrard even the undertakers were on strike. It was not a good day to die.

Much of Paris was shut down, but workers' councils were keeping what was vital running. The occupied power plants kept Paris alight. The radical newspapers were still printed and distributed, urgent telegrams could still be sent, food kept coming into the city, and the gates to the Paris Zoo remained open.

Christopher felt calm. The three of them—Gerrard, Abby, and Daniel—stopped by the wrought-iron fence to look in at the grounds and Chris joined them. They admired the centuries-old botanical garden, Le Jardin des Plantes. Gerrard told them that it had originally been the Royal Medicinal Plant Garden created by King Louis XIII and had survived the revolution. All of them were quiet for a moment as they looked past the gate and at the domes of Gallery of Evolution, and then they opened the gate. Daniel set off running into the open space.

"Slow down," Christopher said. The boy darted forward between flower beds, along the asphalt paths that led to the National Museum of Natural History.

"Speed up!" Gerrard yelled out to the boy in French.

The zoo was to the left, hidden by an avenue of symmetrical and severely clipped trees. Abby put her arm in Christopher's as they walked along this garden avenue, and then insisted that they stop and watch the flamingoes on the other side of the fence that divided the zoo from the rest of the garden. Once through the gate for the zoo they found the place flooded with students. Young people were standing between the caged lion and tiger, staring at tortoises in a rocky tank, and ignoring a yak.

Inside the central building a zookeeper, a plump young man in overalls and a red cap, stood in front of a Plexiglas window and defended the penguins. About six students were shouting at him, and he was holding a ring of keys over his head and shouting back. A girl with long black hair wearing a paisley patterned blouse jumped up and reached for the keys while her friend with his bow tie and slicked-back hair lectured the zookeeper on class consciousness.

The shadows cast down from the hundreds of window frames in the oval skylight overhead graphed the scene. The students repeated the same request again and again, and Gerrard intervened. He approached the zookeeper and was surprised to realize that the man was, in fact, relatively young. He was a fat man, but his round face was taut. The band of his cap was tight around his head, and it left a mark on his forehead that was clearly visible when he removed the cap to wipe his brow. He'd seemed older from a distance, but he was probably in his late twenties or early thirties.

"Are you the only one on duty?" Gerrard asked.

"I'm sorry," the zookeeper said as he turned toward Gerrard. "What was that?"

"Your coworkers are all on strike. You're the only one still working?" Gerrard asked. Hearing this the other students stopped shouting. The zookeeper's face turned bright red. He held up his arms in a gesture of exasperation and started flapping them, moving his forearms up and down like some kind of wounded bird. He didn't say anything right away, but watching his face Gerrard could tell that he was working his way up to it.

"It's a very fine thing," Gerrard interrupted. He turned toward the other students, to a kid in a green sweater and thick glasses. "It's a fine thing that he should be working. What if he weren't? Who would look after these animals if it weren't for this singular zookeeper."

"The animals need me," the zookeeper said to the kid in the sweater.

And Gerrard agreed. Of course the animals needed him. What else could he do but come in to work, clock in, and collect his wage? While the rest of his countrymen fought de Gaulle, set up workers' councils, and stayed out on strike, it was up to him, to this one zookeeper, to focus on something more important: the penguins.

"I have to work. The animals rely on me."

"But why is that?"

"What do you mean?"

Now Gerrard had to be careful. The point was that the animals only needed his support for as long as they remained in their cages. As long as they were in their cages then somebody had to feed them and clean up after them, but why should they stay in there?

"What would you have me do? Let them out of their cages? All of you want me to let them go, but they can't fend for themselves."

"He's right," Gerrard said to the girl in the paisley shirt. She flipped her long black hair out of her face and started to reach up for the zookeeper's keys again. "No really, he's right. What would a giraffe or an Asian elephant do with itself on the streets of Paris?"

"Just think of it," the zookeeper said.

"And yet, you are breaking with the strike, and if you continue this way you'll face more and more pressure. More and more pressure to open the cages as an act of solidarity."

"That would be terrible. The lion? The sea otter? Just where would they go?"

"What you need is to do something symbolic. You need to make a statement," Gerrard said.

"What kind of statement?"

Gerrard paced for a moment in front of the cage, he put his feet in between the lines of shadow on the cement floor making sure to keep them in the light, and tried to communicate thought.

"You see that handsome middle-aged couple over there by the orangutans? He is a man named Christopher Robin Milne and that is his wife, Abby," Gerrard said. He waited in order to let his words sink in.

"Yes?" The zookeeper was interested.

"Christopher Robin is an expert in bears," Gerrard said. All Gerrard was asking for was one key, one animal. If the zookeeper would release a bear into the care of Christopher Robin, could trust a member of Les Détournés to take care of, say, one small black bear, then this would be enough. By turning over one bear to the occupation he would have met his obligation as a worker.

"The bears are very sensitive. They have many needs. They have a special diet."

Gerrard pointed to Christopher and Abby. They'd moved on to the next cage, a room behind glass that appeared to be empty but that on closer examination contained a tiny owl that was roosting on a dead tree branch in the far left corner. Abby waved to Gerrard and the zookeeper waved back.

"Sir Christopher Robin Milne is the son of the author A. A. Milne who famously chronicled many tales of animal adventures in the Ashdown Forest near London. Christopher has a very special understanding of bears. Tell him what the bear needs and I'm sure he'll follow your instructions to the letter."

"Just one bear?"

"One silly old bear."

24

On May 24 Christopher and his family sat in their cramped hotel room letting the grey light outside lull them while they played twenty questions and drank tea. When the window was open they could smell tear gas and hear shouting and running footsteps, so they kept the window closed. From where he was sitting Christopher could see the Eiffel Tower poking up over corrugated tin rooftops with brick chimneys. He closed his eyes and held the image of the tower in his mind.

"Got it," he said.

"Is it an animal?" Daniel asked.

"No."

"Is it a shooting star?" Daniel asked again.

"It's not a shooting star either."

"Is it an animal? Is it a shooting star?"

When Daniel had asked his two questions ten times each Abby put down the newspaper, looked into Christopher's eyes, and made her best guess.

"Was it built for the World's Fair on the one hundredth anniversary of the storming of the Bastille?" she asked.

Earlier that evening they'd turned on the black-and-white television that sat behind cabinet doors in their hotel room and tuned in president de Gaulle's address to the nation. The war hero, or as the students called him "the shit in the bed," had a proposition and a plan for a way out of the conflict. He looked positively Victorian in his kepi and uniform, and while Christopher sensed that the general might be worried, he appeared confident. The French tradition would prevail. Even as the president agreed that the strike was legitimate, that the call for more participation in government was rational, he also asserted that the strike could only be settled by referendum. De Gaulle promised that if the people rejected his legislated fix he would step down from office. Despite this retreat, the core of the man, his enormous but somehow quaint confidence, was evident even in the flickering image on the television screen.

"In industry, in agriculture, at the university, we will expand the role of the citizen of France," de Gaulle said.

"Is it an animal?" Daniel asked. He wanted to play again.

Christopher refused to think of an animal. Instead he thought of a cut-up map of Paris that Gerrard had shown him, a map of the streets of Paris, each section its own island separated from the rest. He considered how each section represented a different idea, a different emphasis, a different bit of history, and wished he still had the map, wished he could make out where Rue du Four figured in the equation. He considered whether it would be de Gaulle or the students who would put the city back together again.

"Is it a shooting star?"

"No," Chris said.

"Is it a shooting star?" Daniel asked.

Abby took advantage of the distraction and began to clear the coffee table. She took the teapot and mugs to the bathroom sink and filled it with water. She left them there, in the bathroom sink, to soak until she could find more detergent.

"Is it a bear?" Daniel asked.

Abby nodded her head at this question, which she apparently thought was a good one. "Is it a bear, Christopher?"

They'd been keeping him in the cellar since he'd come back with them from the Paris Zoo. At first Christopher worried that the beast would destroy the hotel's store of fine and mediocre wines, but by the third day he worried instead that the confined and now sedentary bear was being driven mad by the lack of stimulation. They left a light on for him in the hall outside the storage room, but even so the cellar was dank and dark. Even if Daniel and Abby hadn't insisted, Christopher would've gone down to check on the animal. He had an obligation to the black bear, even if the animal had been forced on him.

The zookeeper had told them the bear was named William.

William moved out of his corner and to the middle of the room, stood in the circle from the flashlight, and reached for the ceiling. The bear let out a low groan as he stretched. Christopher crossed to him, clipped the metal chain to his red leather collar as a leash, and then opened his hand. He fed William a date from his palm and the bear took the food gently, using his tongue instead of his teeth.

Then Daniel opened the green metal canister from the zoo, and tipped it, pouring feed onto the dirty floor of the cellar. The bear ate the mix of dried blue and red berries with yellow fish protein off the floor. William licked away the layer of dirt that had settled on the cellar floor. The bear exposed the white stone, washed it clean with his tongue, and then retreated to the far left corner to lick his paws.

"Is it an animal?" Daniel asked. His high-pitched voice echoed off the stones.

Even though it was late, Christopher took the bear out for a walk down Rue du Four. Daniel went out with him at first, petted the bear on the forehead and then fed the animal some berries and walnuts from a Tupperware bowl. The boy leaned away from the bear and shut his eyes when the snorting and snuffling began, but kept smiling the entire time. He opened his eyes again when William stood up straight and stopped breathing in his face, and then Christopher sent him back inside the hotel. It was dangerous out on the streets.

He took the bear for a walk and even out on the barricades. Out on Boulevard Saint-Germain where students were tossing paving stones and police launching tear gas grenades, the bear was conspicuous. The students and the police both turned to watch as the two of them passed, and as he passed the barricade and then an American Express office, Christopher found himself reciting his father's poetry, first silently, to himself, and then out loud.

"The more it goes, tiddly pom, the more it goes, tiddly pom, the more it goes, tiddly pom, on going. And nobody knows, tiddly pom, just why it grows, just why it goes on growing." Christopher changed the words.

25

That night the students listened to President de Gaulle on their transistor radios and heard his weakness behind each word. All they had to do was turn the dial to disrupt his attempt at placating them. They weren't trying to find another station, there were no other French stations broadcasting—the government had shut them down during the general strike—but were content to stay in between, in static.

Natalie had her dinner in a narrow passageway between two buildings near the School of Fine Arts, at a wood table with steel tins and plastic bags and glass jars on top that was pressed against one brick wall. A boy in a leather jacket was ahead of her, making himself a sandwich by cracking the stale baguette open, spreading mustard, and then pushing in slices of hard cheese. He took a gulp from a canteen and then scooted across the bench, making room for her, and handing her the canteen.

When she looked inside the canteen she saw bread crumbs floating at the top, and for a moment she felt nauseated. Still, she closed her eyes and swallowed. It was easy to imagine that the cheese on the table was made of stone, that everything was false, but she cracked her own piece of bread, put mustard inside along with cheese, and took a bite. She had to take another sip of water from the canteen so that she wouldn't choke before making room on the bench for the next in line.

Out on the street Gerrard closed his eyes and walked with an arm stretched out. He crept along feeling the brick wall in order to keep his bearings.

He needed to sleep, to dream normally. It was a physical need. With his eyes still shut Gerrard walked down the street. He let his hand fall to his side and just made his way blind. When he opened his eyes again time had passed and he was in the middle of a battle. He opened his eyes to see canisters of tear gas and paving stones flying back and forth around him. He stuffed his left hand in the pocket of his tweed jacket, and put his right hand over his eyes to shield his face from the glare of grenade launchings. He pinched his nose shut against the gas, and lurched toward the police line.

The police were life-sized newspaper cutouts, and Gerrard wanted to put his hand through them. He would use scissors to carefully cut along the dotted lines and remove their gas masks and helmets. If he cut the newspaper policemen open he was sure he'd find daylight on the other side.

He only stopped when he felt a hand on his back. Natalie rescued him. She coughed and gagged, blind from the gas, and reached out to him, grabbed the collar of his jacket, and fell. He turned back to find her crashing to her knees. As he helped her back onto her feet, when he put his arm around her shoulder and started back to the barricade, he felt his invincibility, his dream, drain away, through his legs and into the earth.

They didn't have time to talk before a few policemen broke ranks and charged them. The police had their batons out, raised over their heads, and their gas masks down over their mouth and eyes.

"They're going to kill us," Natalie said.

"Yes," Gerrard said.

But, before the policemen reached them they were hit by a barrage of paving stones. The police stopped short. One sat down about a third of the way back, shifted his helmet back and forth, and then took off the helmet and touched his nose. He coughed and spat blood.

Behind the barricade Natalie asked Gerrard if he had wanted to get killed. If that was his intention he should have let her know so she could spare herself so much wasted effort.

"Your dream theory is just a cover story for your self-destruction," she said.

A gas grenade exploded very close by and they felt it. Pinpricks of heat disrupted their conversation and when the air cleared the blast had left someone dead. There was a body at their feet. Gerrard knew him.

Raoul's parents had disowned him after seeing him on television throwing paving stones. Now Raoul had shrapnel in his chest. The dead boy's blood spilled out onto the cobblestones. His eyes didn't move to follow or track where Natalie waved her hand.

All the whispered rumors were now confirmed. Students were mortal and could be killed.

In fact there were many who had disappeared since the first skirmishes on May 3, hundreds of people who'd simply slipped away into the ether not to be heard from again. Some of them, like Raoul, were killed just by being in the wrong place at the wrong time, others were killed in cold blood, made to disappear, and still others had simply had enough and went on vacation to Switzerland or Norway.

There was the blood. The State would kill them if it could, and Natalie and Gerrard saw this and decided to abandon the barricade, abandon their defensive posture.

"That's not right," Gerrard said.

"Is he dead?" Natalie asked.

"Raoul, that dead boy was named Raoul," Gerrard said.

When she'd first been with Gerrard, Natalie had worried about what was rational and what was not. But, at the Paris Stock Exchange she no longer cared. The fact that she was still alive was the only ground she needed to stand on.

There on the Île de la Cité outside Notre Dame they discussed it. What they needed were wine bottles filled with gasoline and the gasoline could be taken directly from the streets, siphoned out of the tanks of automobiles parked along Boulevard Saint-Michel.

As for wine bottles, thirty or forty students, men in sport jackets stained by tear gas and women in mud-stained clothes, debated whether they should steal full bottles from restaurants or go begging for empties, but before they'd decided two older men from Café Charbon, each of them at least thirty, rolled up a wheelbarrow with a mix of both full and empty bottles of Pinot noir, Pinot grigio, and champagne.

It would have been unpatriotic to waste good French wine and they were all drunk by the time the group made it to the other side of the Seine. Natalie and Gerrard found one corked and full and managed to dislodge the cork with a pocket knife, and when they arrived on the Boulevard de Sébastopol Natalie felt light-headed.

This would be a pure act of destruction, to clear the ground to make something new, only Natalie also knew that it was also bringing something forward. There were lines of memory from the gasoline Molotov cocktails and the Stock Exchange.

Natalie reached out to put her hand on Gerrard's back for support, but instead of his shoulders she found air. He'd already started. He slung the first wine bottle filled with gasoline at the Stock Exchange's doors. The Molotov cocktail struck and a fire started between the Greco-Roman columns. Other students, some with axe handles, some with crowbars, climbed the steps on the west. They broke the tall windows, tossed champagne bottles inside, and watched as luxurious carpets and drapes caught fire there.

Natalie glanced down at her feet and found she was standing in mud, but she wasn't worried. The ground beneath her feet was soft, pliable, but still firm enough to stand on.

26

The boy was feeding the bear honey off a long wooden spoon while Abby brushed him with a hairbrush that had once belonged to her mother. It was desecration of a family heirloom and Chris winced each time a bristle came out in the bear's thick fur.

"You want to go back to the bookstore soon, don't you?" Abby asked.

"Of course."

"We'll need to put in another order of the mushroom book," she said.

The bear was always hungry and while Christopher still had half a canister of feed left, it was clear that the current arrangement would not endure much longer.

He reached over and took the hairbrush away from Abby. How had it happened that the mundane trials of his life seemed distant? The bookstore, their drawing room, their television set, always having the right brand of tea on hand, he wanted these things back.

He patted the bear on the neck and watched him lick his lips and use his paw to clean his face. Chris pulled the fur out of the brush.

Abby let her arms dangle at her sides. She lifted her teacup to her lips and then placed it back down without taking a sip.

"Christopher," she started. She took her husband's hand, forced the hairbrush out of his hand and onto the table. It was a solid oak brush with her family crest inscribed on the flat back. "Christopher. I don't want to go back."

Christopher asked how long she thought they could live in a hotel room. For how long did she want to scrounge for meals? For how long would they hold on to this absurd bear and watch it starve? For how long would they be willing to risk getting mauled?

"What kind of life do we have here, Abby? How could this last?"

"I saw a French lady kissing her butcher yesterday," Abby said. "I walked into the shop and found them pressed up against the display case, quite passionate."

"Yes, well the French are quite like that, aren't they?"

What he liked about his habitual life, all the routines, was that it meant that he didn't have to decide all the time. He was free to be uninvolved.

This is why when Gerrard's friend Natalie had tried to seduce him he'd turned her away. She was a stunning young girl, desirable of course, but so very French. He'd turned Natalie away instinctively, not just because he owed fidelity to Abby, but because a tryst would have meant giving up the freedom his habits afforded him and his habits were what sustained him. The habit of walking, the habit of running the bookstore, the habit of loving his wife, this is what he needed.

The bear let out a high-pitched yawn, a yawn that was both a yawn and a whine. Daniel proceeded to feed the bear honey, sticking the wooden spoon in the oversized tin can that stored the stuff, and ladling it out.

"French butcher," Daniel said.

27

You think I am the real Christopher Robin?" Christopher asked.

"Not exactly," Gerrard said. "But maybe you could be a new Christopher Robin."

It was May 27 and they were having some difficulty convincing William to descend into the Metro. Christopher was at the top of the steps, seemingly enjoying the problem, while Gerrard considered the logistics of it. The bear was seated on the third step down, cleaning his paws with his tongue, oblivious to Gerrard's insistent tugging on the chain around its neck. Gerrard tried clicking his tongue, singing "Frère Jacques," cooing, and swearing, but the animal remained unresponsive. Only when Gerrard looped the chain around the railing on the stairwell and used the leverage to pull did the animal take notice. The bear let out an offended roar and swiped the air with its paw.

Christopher Robin let out an involuntary yelp, and it took a while before Gerrard was brave enough to ascend the stairs and maneuver around the bear.

The rumor was that de Gaulle had vanished from France. Some said that he'd fled the country after telling his staff that the game was up, and that he expected that within a few days the communists would be in power, but another rumor was that he had gone to Germany to discuss the situation with General Massu and to determine the reliability of the French troops stationed there. Earlier that day the head of the CGT union had announced that the bosses had met the workers' demands. Pierre Mendès-France had read from a list of concessions from a platform set behind rows of cranes. The workers were to receive big wage increases, pensions, longer vacations, and would be allowed to work shorter hours. This was not enough, however, and the workers had shouted him down. The slogan at the Renault factory was *"Gouvernement populaire!"*

There would be a mass meeting at Charlety Stadium precisely in an effort to enact such a popular government, and because everyone agreed that the strike had come to a turning point. The three of them, Gerrard, Christopher, and the bear, were headed to the stadium in order to intervene. Gerrard felt that if there was an appropriate moment for Christopher to step forward and lead, if there was a time to find a new game, this was it.

"We'll never get him on the train. He's too big," Christopher said.

Gerrard had to agree, but walking from Rue du Four to the stadium would not be easy either, especially since the bear refused to walk in a straight line.

William was too much, an actual black bear who had his own particular ways and history. A young Frenchman attending veterinary school in Toronto had purchased him from a hunter who'd killed William's mother, and after that the bear was an unofficial regimental mascot. However, while he was raised and made tame, he was also wild. There was no way to predict what he might do. William was not a cooperative bear. In fact, it seemed that his familiarity with people just made him disobedient.

"He's hungry," Christopher said.

The animal put his front paw up against the plate glass storefront of a café and grocery. The grocery was closed, but they spotted the owner, a bald man in an apron, huddling under a counter toward the back of the store, peeking up at their bear. Christopher rapped on the glass with his knuckles, repeating the gesture again and again until the shopkeeper finally ventured out and stood, slightly hunched, by the locked door.

"The bear is hungry," Chris said. "Do you have any fish available?" he asked.

"I do not comprehend," the shopkeeper said.

Gerrard put his face up against the glass, pushing his nose against the glass so as to make a pig face at the man. He said, in English, "The bear is angry and will break in to eat unless you give him fish now."

At this the shopkeeper retreated. Gerrard laughed and then grimaced when their pet put a giant paw on his shoulder and proceeded to lick the wax out of Gerrard's ear. The beast's open mouth smelled bad.

The shopkeeper came back to the window with a stack of frozen fish—halibut, trout, and shrimp—wrapped in wax paper and tied together with brown string. He pushed open the door with his foot and dropped the hard cold squares to the sidewalk.

"Here you are, monsieur. Behold, fish!" The bald man disappeared inside again and ducked behind his hanging scale. William set upon his packages, opening them with his teeth, and then sniffed and snorted until all of it was gone behind his sharp, white teeth.

They made their way down Boulevard Saint-Michel, let the warm summer afternoon draw them along until sunset. When they reached the occupied Charlety Stadium the sky was a dark orange color.

Inside the fifty thousand people gathered weren't there for an athletic event; they weren't there to watch anything. There was an anxiety inside the stadium. Steno girls in light blue sweaters, university students in jackets and ties, and long-haired factory boys in blue jeans were all of them waiting to discover something, but the bear was hungry again and he resisted Gerrard's attempt to direct him onto the stage.

"What have I gotten myself involved in?" Christopher asked as he looked out at the crowd.

A girl in a short skirt and a brown leather jacket was running in circles in front of the bleachers and waving a red-and-black flag over her head. She was running laps as if she were performing in the opening ceremonies for an anarchist Olympics, while behind her thousands of students lay about on the field. They were on their backs in the grass, smoking cigarettes, reading newspapers, and listening. The speaker on stage was fairly effective; most of the fifty thousand were held rapt, however a few did turn to look at Christopher and his bear even before William let out a roar.

Gerrard asked if it would be okay if Christopher Robin were to speak, and the three of them waited at the back of the stage for a turn. However, it was but a moment before they were signaled to the microphone.

Christopher reached out to the bear and petted him. He put his fingers in the animal's fur and took a breath as William turned and sniffed him back.

Gerrard stepped up to the microphone. "History has chosen us," he said. "If that sounds like something a politician would say, I'm sorry, but I mean it literally. History has chosen us. Not the grand history of the kings, and of wars, or of dates in textbooks, but rather our own secret histories. The history of our childhood, and our grandparents' childhoods, that's what has chosen us. History has chosen us, chosen us to take part in the creation of memories out of the present."

Gerrard introduced Chris, and a few of the students seemed to recognize his name. They shouted out in English, asked about Pooh and the little pig, and then when Chris and William stepped up to the microphone everyone was quiet. Chris was shaking, and when the black bear leaned over and nudged him with his wet nose Chris laughed and heard his own voice as an alien thing that had been amplified back at him, but despite this Christopher did his best.

"Before my father created the Winnie-the-Pooh stories and before he wrote about a character named Christopher Robin, he wrote for a humor magazine called *Punch*," Christopher said. "My father was quite proud of the writing he did there. And there was a lot about *Punch* that was admirable, quite a lot of skill that went into the magazine, but what was most interesting looking back on it now, perhaps what might be relevant to you as well, is the way in which Punch, not the magazine, but the four-hundred-year-old puppet who was the mascot for the magazine, and Winnie-the-Pooh are the same."

The crowd at Charlety was not one mass of spectators, but was broken into pieces, multiple masses and cliques. There was constant movement, people shuffling back and forth and facing in all different directions. Chris couldn't tell if people were listening to him.

"Punch from Punch and Judy is a puppet who carries a slapstick. Punch throws his baby down the stairs, he beats his wife, he even beats a policeman. Punch pretends to be too simple and stupid to understand what he is doing, and this is how he gets what he wants."

Christopher reached out to pet William, but the bear turned his head away.

"Punch is like Pooh. How? They are both toys, imaginary, and they're both narcissists who always get what they want," Chris said. "The one difference is that Pooh is innocent, whereas Punch is guilty. Pooh is authentic while Punch is a fraud. Pooh really doesn't know what it is he's doing. Punch knows exactly what he is doing.

"My father made his fortune writing children stories. He was a success at *Punch,* but he made history with Pooh. And you should all ask yourselves why. It's not just a question that is significant for me. These stories were wildly popular all across the globe. Why?

"The truth is that my father didn't particularly admire children. He thought that children were charming enough, the way that puppies or kittens might be charming, but they were not interesting to him. More to the point, he felt there was nothing truly good about children. Pooh, for instance, is lovable but not because his motives are noble. What makes Pooh admirable is that his motives are undisguised. Pooh isn't good at covering his own tracks. He isn't clever, or even competent, and that is his secret strength and charm.

"The way my father thought of Pooh, this is how de Gaulle

thinks of you. The myth of your innocence is what is supporting you, and de Gaulle thinks you've just been lucky so far. You are children, and as such you are guileless. Too many of you think the same way he does.

"In one of my father's Pooh stories, one about an expedition, I organize a search for a stick, maybe for Punch's slapstick. In the story I claim the stick is the North Pole. I get all of my imaginary friends together, all the puppets and toys, and we set off through the Hundred Acre Wood looking for it, and along the way Pooh gets hungry. He wonders when we'll have time to stop for a little smackerel of something. He stumbles into a gorse bush. And, what else happens? Many things, mostly small and unpleasant things. The piglet becomes quite concerned about being ambushed by Heffalumps, for example. The donkey complains that he's forgotten to bring thistles to eat, and, oh yes, the important thing is that a little baby kangaroo falls into a stream and nearly drowns.

"And in the story it is this last calamity that inspires Pooh. Pooh manages to find the North Pole just at the moment when it's needed most and he holds it across the stream so that the little kangaroo will drift up to it and be able to rescue himself. Pooh finds the North Pole, but he doesn't realize what he's found.

"This is how the Gaullists understand your story. This is how they think you have discovered power. They think it's just been an accident. You found something that was momentarily useful to you, it happened to be power, but given how clumsy and how inept you are you won't be able to hold on to it for long.

"Listen. I'm not Christopher Robin from the storybooks. I am Christopher Milne who is a veteran of the war against the fascists and Nazis. This bear isn't Pooh from my father's stories. This Pooh has fangs and claws.

"Punch and Pooh are both fictions. They're both of them a kind of puppet and the only way a puppet can pull his own strings is by being just as clever and remorseless as he has to be.

"Paris is a Hundred Acre Wood," Chris said. "We need to find the North Pole."

When Christopher descended from the platform the crowd moved quickly to get out of the way. He started toward the exit and the crowd parted for him.

Gerrard caught up to Chris, but the boy didn't seem to have anything useful to say. There was no help there. Chris had to decide what came next on his own, and he did. He turned and addressed the crowd following him.

"We are looking for the North Pole," he said.

When Christopher stepped away from the platform and into the mud the students moved out of his way. He wanted to make the ground firm again and so he guided William between the rows and the crowd parted around them. A few of the students must've understood his English, a few must have known of his father's stories, because people were falling in behind him and following him as he led them.

Christopher set off on an expotition from Charlety Stadium.

At first Gerrard felt disoriented and was glad to let Chris lead, but after a while he regretted this because Chris took a wrong turn somewhere and in his disorientation he must've lost track of time because in what seemed like a very short while they weren't anywhere along Boulevard Jourdan but had arrived at Jardin du Luxembourg.

The bear pulled them to an apiary behind a white picket

fence. First he'd stopped at the entrance, by the wrought-iron gates. He'd stood up on his hind legs and let out a roar that turned into a yawn. Christopher had abandoned any effort to control the bear, and just let William pull him this way and that, but everyone followed along, about two hundred students and workers, as Christopher was dragged down a wide path of mud between two neatly trimmed lawns and around the Fountain of the Observatory, and to a pavilion tucked behind tall bushes in the Jardin du Luxembourg.

The man-made beehives were constructed out of stained oak, designed for public display, and all of them stood by impotently as the bear smashed one after another. The ground was littered with green copper roofs from the wooden beehives, and William licked his paws. The bear ate wax and honey and ignored the bees swarming around him, but one crawled onto Gerrard's collar, walked to the front of his neck, just above his collar and beneath his Adam's apple, and impaled him with its stinger.

Christopher pulled on the bear's chain, and Gerrard tried to help him. They both of them pulled as hard as they could. Gerrard's neck and face began to sweat.

A student twirled his arms, spinning back and slipping into the grass.

A few more students helped them pull William away from the honey and eventually they managed to get back onto the mud path and set out in a new direction.

"Christopher, people are complaining that you did not say anything about bees before," Gerrard said.

"Tell them," Chris said. "Tell them that I apologize. Those were entirely the wrong sorts of bees."

Gerrard translated for the crowd.

Eventually William brought them to the Eiffel Tower. Gerrard walked under the structure and looked up, craned his head back and examined the latticework, the iron beams and square platforms.

"I should have guessed," Christopher said.

"How do you mean?" Gerrard asked.

"It's the North Pole. Pretty obvious, don't you think?" Christopher asked.

Gerrard looked up into the tower again, at the iron girders and rivets. The Eiffel Tower was a kind of clock. It was the kind of clock that broadcast time as well as measured it. The State broadcast television and radio signals and created time. If you were French you could tune in the Eiffel Tower, tune in the ORTF, to find out what that, what being French, meant.

Christopher asked if anyone had poster board and spray paint on hand, and was soon surrounded by a multicolored array of options.

"North Pole. Discovered by thousands with the help of a bear." Christopher sprayed black paint on a rectangle of plywood. Christopher sat down on the cement and whistled to William. He leaned forward and whispered in the beast's ear. Gerrard could just make it out.

"You're some bear," Christopher said. He ran his hand between William's furry ears.

Gerrard sat down next to him and reached out for the bear, but William moved away. Gerrard stood up and took a step toward the bear, and William stood up on his hind legs and showed Gerrard his teeth.

"Do you know how to do a reality check?" Gerrard asked.

"What's that?"

Gerrard told Christopher to check his watch and see if the hands ticked forward clockwise in the usual way. He told Christopher to try reading a newspaper or a book to see if the text held its meaning.

Standing under a TV antenna, under the monster, the smokestack, called the Eiffel Tower, Gerrard realized he'd fallen for a trap. He thought Christopher could fit the pieces together, but everything was even more fragmented. He'd meant to derail Christopher Robin, and to participate in the derailing of the city, but as the crowd of students mingled around him, some of them still carrying broken cobblestones, it seemed as though all Gerrard had managed to derail was himself.

Some students had musical instruments—bongo drums, horns, and what sounded like ukuleles—and they were playing "La Marseillaise" very fast. They were singing the lines in a jokey way, emphasizing the wrong words.

"Grab your weapons, citizens! Form your battalions! Let us march! May impure blood water our fields!"

They'd shifted everything around, history had been deconstructed, and now they stood at the North Pole and surveyed the blankness.

Gerrard turned away from the ukuleles and drums, the big black bear, and from the sound of the fountains in the Champ de Mars. All of it stopped. The moment froze, and then the smell of asphalt and moisture, the smell of the city and with it the feeling of being located in real space, evaporated. Everything was still.

Champ de Mars disappeared, the Seine evaporated, and the world was left flat and grey and unmarked. Beyond the foundation of the tower the ground was made of mud or clay. Gerrard, Christopher, and the students were still on the concrete foundation of the tower, iron girders interlocked overhead, but the rest of the built world disappeared.

Gerrard had thought the dreamtime was a land outside of history, outside of the realm of cause and effect, that it was the eternal space behind the contingent space of everyday life, but the dream was just what was broadcast from the tower. It wasn't eternal but was, in fact, exactly the contingent everyday life everyone wanted to wake up from. There was a black light in the Eiffel Tower, and this light kept everyone asleep, but Christopher Robin and the students had finally extinguished that black light.

Daniel Cohn-Bendit approached them. He moved slowly, trembling as he stepped past William. Cohn-Bendit had an electrically amplified bullhorn in his hands, and he held it out to Christopher.

"We would like it if you would explain what is happening," he said to Christopher. Christopher just shrugged.

Gerrard got down on his hands and knees. The Earth was made of grey clay, but the moon was out and the lights in the Eiffel Tower were still getting electricity from somewhere. Christopher took the bullhorn.

Gerrard looked out at the crowd. He looked over their heads at the stars. The sky was a façade.

Christopher Robin let out a breath, a small whistle. "This is the North Pole," he said. "And I am going to throw a party here." Christopher hesitated. "It's to be a special sort of party, a party to celebrate what you did when you did what you did to occupy the factories, what you did when you did what you did to occupy your lives."

Christopher let go of the button on the bullhorn and turned to look at Gerrard. "Is that right?" he asked.

Gerrard didn't answer, because that was the moment when he spotted Natalie in the crowd. At first Gerrard wasn't sure it was her; he wasn't sure he'd seen anyone at all. Christopher called out for volunteers who might want to loot the tower for items that would be useful for a tea party, and Natalie stepped forward.

"Where did it go?" she asked them.

"Where did what go?" Christopher asked.

"Paris," she said.

Back at the hotel Abby opened the hotel casement window, swinging the left side in and then sitting at the mahogany table and enjoying the view of street lamps and wet cobblestones below. The city was reflected in the leaded glass panels in a fractured way, appearing on the panels between the brass frames. Daniel had adopted half a baguette as his new favorite toy and was wandering from room to room with it, apparently telling the loaf a story about big black bears and wooden-topped men who lived inside the television set. Daniel lost his top right incisor that morning, but there was no talk of a tooth fairy. Such compensation hardly seemed necessary. The loss of his tooth, normally the kind of traumatic event that would've sent Daniel into one of his fits, was simply noted by a few recitations of the Woodentops opening theme, and then forgotten. The fantasy that Paris had become was manna for Daniel. The boy's smile was a facial fixture now.

"Mama, when will Papa be back?" Daniel asked.

"He didn't say, Daniel."

"I was hoping he would read me a story, perhaps one of Grandfather's, or maybe a French story. A fairytale," Daniel said.

"I'll read to you, darling. In fact, we should draw you a bath now. It's nearly time for bed."

Daniel put his loaf of bread on the table and went to the bath and turned on the faucet there. She was certain that Daniel seemed better in Paris than he'd ever been in Dartmouth. It was unexpected, as he was a child who required his routine to be rigidly maintained. In fact, on top of the rest of the strangeness that had come along with his birth, the little anomalies that bothered Christopher so much, the rituals Daniel engendered, and all the other disturbances that had culminated in this trip to Paris, her son's new coherence was unsettling in itself.

"Daniel? Are you in the bath already?" she asked the now closed door.

Abby stood up from the dark wood table and went to prepare tea. The French tea she'd found was a loose mix of assam and little bits of flowers and lavender, but it had a nice kick. When the electric kettle sounded, however, Abby found that adding hot water to the mix produced something like mud in her teacup.

She wanted to check on him, not because she'd heard anything, not because he needed help, but because she needed him, needed his reassurance.

"I think I'm the wrong Daniel," he said through the door.

"Are you all right, dear?" she asked. She'd left her teacup on the table by the window and pressed her ear to the bathroom. When she pulled away from it, she found on the right side of her face, from her ear to her chin, a crescent-shaped mud stain. The mud had to have come from somewhere, but when she looked at the door it appeared clean. She reached out to it, touched the frame, and her fingers sank into what should have been hard wood or plaster.

"I think I'm the wrong Daniel Milne. There might be more than one, mightn't there?"

"Daniel?" She put her ear to the door again, not minding the invisible dirt there, and while she listened for her son, she glanced back toward the window and noticed that the streetlight had gone out. In fact, from where she was standing it looked as though all of Paris had grown dark.

Daniel opened the bathroom door, pulling it into the bathroom so Abby almost stumbled forward, and then stepping out with dripping hair and wet pajamas. He had not remembered to dry himself with a towel, and water was dripping onto the wood floor.

"If I were different, if I were the wrong Daniel, how would you know?" he asked.

She reached past him and took a towel from the back of the bathroom door, but while it was neatly folded it was covered in mud.

"Daniel, you should hold my hand now," Abby said.

"Why is that?"

"Just take my hand," she said. But as Daniel, perhaps the right Daniel but perhaps not, reached for her, the light inside the hotel room blinked out and they were in the dark. Abby reached for her son and found mud.

Wherever Abby placed her hand she touched mud and even this seemed insubstantial. She tried again, kneeling in the dark, and found wet dirt under her fingers, a loam that sifted easily and got caught beneath her fingernails. This was no more substantial than the simple mud she'd been sinking in before, but there was a difference.

"Is this the wrong mud?" Daniel asked.

He was somewhere nearby, but in the dark Abby was wary of naming possibilities. She was not even particularly confident that they were still in their hotel room.

In fact, they were not in their hotel room any longer but were standing at the edge. The edge of precisely what was as yet unclear, but Abby could see where the landscape ended and the horizon began. But now her eyes were adjusting, and perhaps there was some light after all. Not in the sky, but somewhere behind her, while in front of her there was a screen or a matte painting. Only instead of a sunset or a French promenade the screen displayed nothing but a light brown film.

"Daniel?" She called out for her son and then found him standing next to her. He took her by the hand and they turned to look at the source of the light.

The Eiffel Tower was a beacon. Abby, Daniel, and all the other people left behind—the butcher and his lover, policemen in kepis, Raoul and the girls from Nanterre, hundreds of anonymous people—stood huddled at the edge of the world. They were all facing the centre, turned toward the Eiffel Tower, and all of them were hoping it would hold together.

The network of lattices in the Eiffel Tower cast shadows on the steps in front of Natalie, but when she looked around she couldn't tell where the light was coming from. Paris was pitch-black; the world had been erased.

She was still carrying her book with her but it was of little solace now because she wasn't quite sure where the book ended and she began. It seemed to her that she herself might be something that had been derailed, a quote or a character from somewhere else. She was someone who had been derailed.

She'd volunteered to loot the Eiffel Tower. She was supposed to bring back wine, to help carry down chairs and round dining tables, but once she started up she stepped away from the others. She hoped to see something more, find something that was still out there in some real part of the city, if she climbed to the top.

When she was little she'd been a sleepwalker. When she was five she'd had her recurring dream about radio stars. Edith Piaf, Léo Ferré, and Maurice Chevalier came to visit her. She dreamed they were waiting outside the heavy green doors of her apartment building in Le Marais, waiting for her to bring down her orange Peugeot tricycle so she could ride with them down the narrow streets to the place where songs were. Natalie woke up many times to find herself dragging her tricycle. The clatter from bumping it down the spiral steps would usually wake her up before she reached the ground floor, or if the noise didn't wake her it woke her parents.

Natalie had been a sleepwalker, but she'd only made it out those front doors and onto the cobblestones once. Her parents found her sitting on her tricycle. Her feet were on the pedals but she wasn't pedaling. Instead they found her singing "Non, Je Ne Regrette Rien" softly under her breath while men and women in fine clothes tried to ignore her. They stepped around the little girl whose presence didn't make sense. After that Natalie's parents put a chain lock on the front door. They made sure it was placed high on the door, above her reach.

Natalie looked down the stairs at the pillars and lattice of steel bars and tried to remember what it had been like to remember her dreaming.

She'd been maybe four years old when she dreamed that her father confessed to being a wind-up toy. She couldn't have been more than four. He was just like the painted cowboy toy on her dresser. He told her that he'd been built in Japan and he made a whirring sound, a series of mechanical clicks, and then he told her that she was sleeping. He told her that she was dreaming.

Now, climbing the Eiffel Tower at the behest of Christopher Robin, Natalie turned again to look out at Paris and again the horizon was blank.

She opened Sagan's book and read the last few lines:

When I am in bed, at dawn, listening to the cars passing below in the streets of Paris, my memory betrays me. . . . Something rises in me that I call by name, with closed eyes. Bonjour, tristesse!

All she had with her now were memories of tin fathers, trips to amusement parks where she would ride carousels and look at her own reflection in the mirrored glass at the centre of the wheel, and pop songs from ORTF. She could remember a hundred different fantasies, but nothing that was real.

Natalie reached the top of the tower and there was still nothing. She stood at the rail and looked out into darkness.

The students from Nanterre and the Sorbonne brought down small round tables from Café Brébant on the second floor. They brought down carafes of wine, tea pots, pastries, and cakes. Christopher Robin sat down and William stood next to the table. Christopher Robin poured himself a cup of tea, and William snapped his jaws and gulped down the Napoleon pastry when Christopher Robin tossed it to him.

Guy Debord, Isadora Baris, and Daniel Cohn-Bendit sat with them at the table. Isadora poured out red wine, and Guy leaned back and looked around at the blank disc around the tower. Cohn-Bendit bit into a pastry.

Meanwhile, the students kept on looting the tower. They

emptied the restaurant on the top floor; they brought out finery and set it down in the clay mud. The students and workers sat around tables with pristine white tablecloths and drank champagne from bottles and used their fingers to eat from tins of caviar and jam.

"A long, long time ago, in the beginning, there were no people, no trees, no plants," Isadora said to Guy as she offered up her wineglass for a toast. "There was nothing."

Christopher Robin put down his cup of tea and reached over to pet William, but unclipped the leash from the bear's collar instead. William moved out from under the tower and across the clay. William made a path in the soft earth as he ran. Christopher Robin couldn't tell how far away William was because there was nothing else there to give him a sense of perspective. Eventually William stopped and scratched his hindquarters with his mouth. The bear bent and licked between his legs, and then scuttled on.

When Christopher Robin's father wrote his autobiography in 1938 he entitled the book *It's Too Late Now*. The book was sold to the publishers as a literary autobiography. The famous author of the Pooh stories had promised the publishers that he'd tell the story of how he became an author, but the book was nothing like that at all. Instead of writing about all the famous people who had helped him along the way, instead of regaling readers with stories of excess and debauch in the halls of *Punch*, his father had mostly turned his effort toward remembering what it had been like to be young.

At the North Pole the moon was painted onto the sky. There was no light coming from the stars or moon, but there was light. Chris could see white electric light at the edges of the sky.

Why had his father written the Pooh stories? Why had the esteemed A. A. Milne created a fictional Christopher Robin in the place of his real son? It had been a way to escape from being fifty, a way to return to the source of his life.

Maybe there was a spotlight behind the façade at the horizon? Maybe there was something real? It couldn't all be dreamtime, could it? It couldn't be flat clay forever in all directions.

The rule Christopher's father never spoke aloud but always insisted upon was this: Never grow up. Enjoy the trivial aspects of life, remain innocent, stay where you are. It was a rule that was impossible to obey, a rule that could never be spoken of directly, but it persisted.

There were two poles: childhood and adulthood. There was innocence and there was corruption. All through his life Christopher Robin had rebelled against his father by siding with corrupted adulthood, by refusing innocence and joy, but this was just playing the same game in reverse.

His own father knew that the child was innocent only in so much as he or she was visibly corrupt. His father argued that adulthood could be more joyful than childhood precisely through the abandonment of this sort of corrupted innocence. So how was it that Christopher continued to turn away from his fictional counterpart? Wasn't his effort to be real, authentic, mature just exactly his attempt to remain a child?

"We've run out of wine," Guy said. He tipped his glass over and the tiny bit of red wine that was left in his glass dribbled onto the white tablecloth.

There was nothing in Paris and Christopher Robin realized it. There was nothing here for him, and he resolved to bring this nothing back with him when he returned to his adulthood in Dartmouth.

What surprised Gerrard was that he wasn't surprised. From the beginning Gerrard had known what was coming. He'd set up the dreamtime, helped Christopher Robin find the North Pole, and now he had to ask himself if that was all there was to it. Gerrard had derailed Christopher Robin, Paris, and from the looks of it the rest of the world, but he'd only arrived at the place from which he'd set out from the start.

Guy Debord rose and sat down and said, "Thank you," which was the proper thing to say, and then Debord shut his eyes again, but every now and then he shook his head and said, "I'm not getting it right."

"Christopher Robin," Gerrard said. "I believe we needed to dig."

Christopher Robin was still looking out at the empty world with his chin in his hands. He responded with a shrug, and then wondered if this counted as nothing, which was his favorite thing to do, or if this thing he was doing was a kind of something. Christopher said that while it was indeed very little, almost nothing, on the other hand it was something. In fact, Christopher thought that whenever one set out for nothing one was likely to end up with something instead, but that something might be a little more pleasant, a little more like nothing than most of the nothings one had encountered before.

Gerrard knocked the table over. He first slowly pulled the tablecloth, and was satisfied when the red wine spilled and ran across the linen surface and left a dark stain there. And when the table toppled over and the wineglasses and pastries landed in the mud, that was even better. Gerrard broke a wooden leg off the table and with it scratched out a line in the mud.

In the Pooh story when Christopher Robin found the North Pole, when he sat at a table with Pooh and celebrated finding it, what had happened next was that the story had ended. Christopher Robin had told Pooh that he was going to be growing up, that he couldn't do nothing anymore, and that instead he (Christopher Robin) would be doing some sort of something which meant that Pooh would have to do something about the nothing without Christopher.

Gerrard's father had read him this part about something and how it turns into nothing, about how Christopher Robin would grow up to be an old man and forget about the nothing, and how even the bear would grow old, he'd be ninety-nine before he turned hundred. Gerrard's father had read this to him when he was a very little boy, and then Gerrard's father had become nothing himself. He'd turned himself into nothing, and that was why Gerrard had to dig. In order to get to what wouldn't turn into nothing he had to dig through the story he was in, get past or below Christopher Robin, the Eiffel Tower, and the strikes of May 1968, to the real thing underneath.

And so Gerrard dug a hole.
He
dug
and he
dug
and he
dug
and as he
dug
he sang "The Internationale."

So comrades, come rally,
And the last fight let us face.
The Internationale,
Unites the human race.

Then he dug a little further . . . and a little further . . . and then just a little further, and before too long Gerrard heard a

CRACK!

Oh, help? he thought. And then Gerrard fell through the hole he had made.

PART THREE

In which Daniel finds Gerrard in a traffic jam, Natalie stops reading Bonjour Tristesse, *Gerrard tries to wake up, and Christopher Robin invents a new game*

28

Chris looked for Gerrard at the Jardin des Plantes with Abby and Daniel on May 28. The shadow from the skylight at the Paris Zoo broke the cement floor of the main hall into uniform boxes, and crossing the space between the cages meant crossing hundreds of intersecting lines and compartments.

Neither Gerrard nor the zookeeper was anywhere to be seen, but Louis the orangutan was waiting for them. The placard outside the cage informed zoo visitors that Louis was twenty-seven years old. The orangutan climbed down the wide trunk of a sawed-off tree trunk they'd mounted in his cage. Louis found his large corrugated cardboard box that was half-buried in sawdust, walked to the far left corner, and placed the box over his head.

"Hello, Bear," Daniel said.

Christopher tried to smile, but he felt more unsettled than amused. When the orangutan disappeared into the box, all they could see were the animal's prehensile toes. Christopher stepped forward, past the chain, and knocked against the bars of the cage with his knuckle. He called out to the animal, tried to get the ape to come out from hiding, but got no response.

Abby clung to her purse in the monkey house. Her usually perfectly styled auburn hair hung loose around her face and her mouth was a straight line. She was observing everything but not responding much to what she saw.

"I feel as though there is a gap," Abby said as she directed Daniel to look up at the baby orangutan climbing a rope near the chain link around the skylight. The younger orangutan seemed happier than the older one who'd hidden himself away in a cardboard rectangle. "I can ask myself questions that are impossible to answer, like how did I get here from where I was last. How much can I really remember about the process of getting here to the zoo? It seems like there are just moments and I find myself in them from time to time, but most of what goes on happens in darkness."

"Maybe seeing the gap, recognizing how much goes on in darkness, is enough?" Christopher asked. "Can you live with that?"

Abby took him by the hand but didn't answer. They looked for Gerrard outside. The day they'd come to the zoo with Gerrard had been a popular day, but this time they didn't see anyone else there at all. There was nobody to ask for directions, and so they set off in a rather indecisive way, and then stopped and turned around.

At the lizard house the walls were painted green and the heat lamps let off a green light. There were lizards and crocodiles and tarantulas and so on, and Christopher looked down at a salamander in a metal dish of water, looked at the brown pebbles. The animal stuck his tongue out and then climbed out of his dish of water. Christopher knocked on the glass and the salamander scurried away to hide in the sand.

Daniel liked the hippo standing behind an iron gate in an outdoor pen. When they looked through the gate at the grey beast it opened its mouth to show them its pink maw. At the pen for the giraffes Abby watched the animals chew and swallow leaves. And all the penguins looked the same to her.

They did not find Gerrard, but the zookeeper was with the elephants. He had one of the elephants' feet on his lap and was using a meter-long file to remove dead skin and caked-on dirt. Christopher waved to the rotund young man and then waited for the zookeeper to finish what he was doing and approach the bars of the cage.

"Have you seen the boy I was here with the other day?" Christopher asked.

"Can't say that I have," the zookeeper said.

"Oh, I should probably apologize," Christopher said.

"For what, sir?"

"Not only did I lose my friend but I also lost your bear. I took him on a long walk, and he got away from me. He got away from me at the Eiffel Tower."

The zookeeper tapped the elephant file against the bars and chewed on his bottom lip. He kicked at an empty red-and-white-striped box that some unconscionable patron had left just inside the cage, tried to send the cardboard box through the gap between the bars, but missed. Then the zookeeper looked up at Christopher and smiled.

"It's all right," he said. "I know where William is." He led Christopher to the bear's cage, next to the gazelle and the ostrich, and there was no doubt about it. There was William behind the bars.

"Where did you find him?" Christopher asked.

"Monsieur, I found him this morning in the same exact place you see him now. He was right here in his cage when I came in this morning. I guess he got lonely for it." The zookeeper walked toward the cage and held out an apple for William, coaxed him over to the bars, and then dropped the fruit into the animal's mouth. William stood up on his hind legs, stuck his front paws through the bars, rested them on a horizontal bar, and opened his mouth for more.

"May we?" Christopher said. The zookeeper gave Daniel the next apple, and the boy stepped forward to William and gave it to him. The bear crunched it twice with his teeth and then swallowed it down. Abby petted the bear's head, rubbed behind an ear, and then finally smiled.

"That's some bear," Christopher said.

The zookeeper agreed.

On May 30 Natalie was looking for Gerrard in the Latin Quarter when she got to the Champs-Élysées and found the end of the occupations, the end of May, instead. The other half of France (the socialites, business owners, bureaucrats, and right wing students from the Sorbonne) were marching against her, row by row.

The Gaullists were in the streets, and there were thousands and thousands of beautiful people all around her. It was a procession of the moneyed and the comfortable, and nobody was breaking a sweat. The revolution of the leisure classes smelled good.

A pretty young student with black hair, wearing a day dress patterned after a Mondrian painting, blue and white squares divided by perfect black lines, marched with a hundred others behind the banner of the French flag. She held up the front page of the newspaper *France Soir* and chanted the headline: "De Gaulle says, 'I remain! I keep Pompidou.'"

Even as she reached Arc de Triomphe she found row after row of affluent anger and well-coifed reaction but she continued on, walking against the march, hoping somehow to stop it. She walked against the flow of strolling protesters still hoping she might find Gerrard there or that she might find something, at least. France seemed no longer to be dreaming, to be waking up or going back to sleep, but Natalie was seeking some way to be lucid. She stopped walking, stood still under the sea of tricolor flags. Men in Yves St. Laurent sunglasses and clean wool coats shouted that they wanted to liberate the factories from the communists and give the people back the freedom of work. An older woman wearing the same red silk dress in which Donald had dressed Natalie on the night of the barricades put her hand to her neck and grasped her pearls in a protective gesture as she passed Natalie.

Natalie stopped and turned in a slow rotation, scanning the scene that circled round the Place de l'Étoile. The revolution had already been turned around. The students and workers wanted to liberate politics by following their desires. They wanted to take power, but instead their desires had been liberated from politics, and established power had taken the form of their protest away from them as well.

On June 4 Christopher led his family through the traffic jam and looked for an entrance to the Metro, a way back to England. He didn't want to see Paris put itself back together, but he couldn't

cut between the automobiles and through the exhaust fast
enough. Daniel dawdled behind them, the duffle bag the boy
was carrying continually slipping from his shoulder.

Paris was overrun with Minis, compacts, four-door sedans,
and station wagons. The cars were brightly colored, and reflected green, red, and yellow up and down Rue du Four, down
Boulevard Saint-Germain, all along the Seine.

The workers had had their Ascension, but now it was Pente-
cost. Reality descended and the unions made the decision to allow the petrol to return to the gas stations or, putting it another
way, to push workers in the petrol industry back to work so that
the French could drive on their long weekend.

"Artificially flavored and new," Daniel said. He dragged William's leash behind him as he drifted back and forth on the sidewalk. Daniel missed the bear.

"Election. Solution. Election," Daniel echoed.

"We could stay one more day," Abby said. "We could keep
looking?" Abby asked.

Christopher jumped up and down, not looking for Gerrard
anymore but a way through. They'd made it to the river, and even
if that wasn't where they'd meant to go Christopher would be
damned before he retraced his steps. But when they found themselves by the railroad tracks, when Abby stopped to lean on the
stone wall between the Milnes and the water, Christopher finally spotted Gerrard. He was on Pont des Arts, crossing over
from the Louvre. He was half-covered in mud and stumbling
across the bridge in the fashion of a mad derelict. He reached
out to passersby, seeming to offer something he was holding to
each one of them.

They waited for Gerrard on the Left Bank, stood staring at
the dome of the Institut de France, at the black and yellow

stones. They stood blinking against the sun, and Christopher's stomach flipped when he realized what Gerrard was bringing them. Gerrard had one of the stuffed animals with him.

"Here it is," Gerrard said when he stepped up to them. He had a stuffed donkey with him. "I brought this back for you."

Gerrard looked terrible. His sports jacket was ripped up the back, his face was pale, and his eyes were bloodshot. Gerrard took a breath, inhaled deeply, and then let it out. "It's a Heffa-lump," Gerrard said. And then he lurched forward and Christopher had to catch him.

Back at the hotel the desk clerk seemed a little surprised to see Christopher and his family again. Gerrard sat down on a threadbare Louis XIV chair and closed his eyes.

Daniel approached Gerrard, put his hand on his arm, and then poked him on his cheek with his thumb. Daniel pressed hard and when nothing happened he leaned over and put his ear next to Gerrard's mouth.

"He's yawning," Daniel said. "He's sleeping."

The three Milnes worked together to get Gerrard onto their shoulders and into the elevator. When Daniel pressed the button to make the elevator go up, Gerrard startled and stood up on his own, supporting his own weight, but then he fell back. His head snapped back and cracked one of the square mirror panels on the elevator wall. Only slightly cushioned by the arms of Abby and Christopher, both of whom reacted too slowly, Gerrard slipped to the floor of the elevator and began to snore.

The window beside the hotel bed was open. Gerrard had thrown the sheets to the floor but even in the cool air he was still warm, sweating into the mattress. He was in the Milnes' bed and had been asleep for nearly sixteen hours. Natalie stood beside him there, watching him sleep, and then unbuttoned her slacks. She pulled her sweater off over her head, removed the T-shirt underneath, and gathered up the rumpled sheets. She lay down next to him on the bed.

Lying there on a bare mattress and staring at the yellow ceiling at the nineteenth-century light fixtures and elegant molding along the walls, Natalie realized that she was in an empty space, an interstice between the life she'd been born into and a possibility. The hotel bedroom was a limbo, a point or respite between the private and the public. It was not truly neutral, but a space that served to connect the two realms that structured economic and material life of a society that she was attempting to reject. And yet, lying there next to Gerrard, feeling a draft pass over her bare skin, she felt the moment, the space, was open.

She was in bed. That was familiar and defined. A bed was a place for sleep, a place for sickness, and theoretically a space for sex. Natalie had never had sex in a bed—at nineteen, she was barred from the bed as a conventional sexual space. For her, sex was an act squeezed into an automobile, behind a bulge in the lawn of Parc Montsouris, and once in a coat closet.

According to Debord a real revolution had to be total. If the goal was to liberate, to realize desire, this would require redefining the space people occupied in their everyday lives. Natalie wondered how a liberated bed, a redefined spring mattress, might function? How would she interact with a liberated bed? Where would she find it?

Natalie imagined that a liberated mattress would be larger than the 190-centimeters-long rectangle that she was currently occupying. A free sleep would have to include many people. It would be a public form of sleep. She imagined a long hall with a soft floor. A liberated bed would include sheets that stretched for meters. The students and workers would curl up together on a long mattress in a university or factory hall and then there would be collective dreams.

When she considered the bed she was in, the little mattress in the Milnes' hotel room, and tried to connect the experience of this bed to her desire, she realized that a public sleep presented many problems. Her memories of sheets and blue comforters, of times spent drowsing on pillows, or private moments of lazy wakeful connection to the stillness of sleep did not fit the imagined pleasure of a collectivized bed. The bed blankets she'd known had been shields against light and against time. Sleep was a quiet solipsistic peace. What she enjoyed was the memory of the singular odor of her own pillow.

In childhood the benefit of a bad cold, for instance, had been the escape it offered. Chest congestion meant that she would get to lie on her left side, hang half off her little mattress, and feel the warm steam from a humidifier on her face. Warm steam, damp sheets, and a hazy in-between space defined the pleasure to be found in the sick bed.

How could she liberate a bed? Natalie remembered the strange clowns and little men in two-cornered hats that had populated her childhood dreams. She tried to remember the spaces these dream characters had occupied. What sort of landscapes supported the devilish midgets who'd spoken to her when she was six? There hadn't been any ground. Her dreams were empty spaces.

Gerrard was sleeping and she was awake. Gerrard was fully dressed, sweating in his clothes, and she was naked and growing cold.

She shivered in the cool air and wondered what sort of future she might build. What sort of future could they create that could hang in midair and support itself without a foundation? Just who was she now? She no longer felt herself to be a university student, and while she was in bed with her former lover, she could not imagine herself as Cecile. She closed her eyes and tried to imagine herself as a young wife. She pictured herself sitting at a breakfast table, a clean white Formica circle with chrome trim, and imagined pouring milk into a coffee bowl and sipping from it, but she couldn't taste anything.

Natalie rolled over onto her left side and examined him. A rectangle of sunlight illuminated his mouth and chin. His nose cast a shadow. Looking at him, considering Gerrard as a sleeping object, she jerked with a start to realize that his eyes were open.

Gerrard was awake, looking back at her, but she couldn't make out anything meaningful in his gaze.

"What time is it?" he asked.

"It's two o'clock in the afternoon."

"Is it still May?"

"June."

Gerrard closed his eyes again and soon enough his breathing changed again and sleep returned to him. Natalie took his hand in hers and closed her eyes. She imagined that she was sick with a cold, that she was asleep. She imagined that she'd found a truly liberated bed.

29

Gerrard opened his eyes and saw that he was by the administrative building, under a cement overpass that connected to the factory on one side and the administrative building on the other. There was a poster printed in full color stuck to the front door, an advertisement for a Renault Dauphine. The poster displayed a clean white car on the edge of a perfectly blue lake, and a happy family with fishing poles. The family members were to the left of the car, too far away for their faces to be seen, but Gerrard assumed that they were smiling. Sunshine and health and whitewall tires. The poster was selling a completeness or harmony belied by the grim bricks of the factory, the unwashed windows, the strike itself.

He was sleeping and wanted to wake up, but Gerrard couldn't remember when he'd gone to bed. Where would he find himself if he did wake up? Who would he be?

In the dream it was June 7 in 1968 and workers of all types—factory workers, students, professors, grocery clerks, taxi drivers, store clerks, waiters—were gathered outside the Renault automobile factory. The space between the concrete factory itself and the smaller brick administrative building was jammed with people on strike.

Natalie covered the poster of the Renault Dauphine with a flyer on yellow paper—a simple line drawing of a clenched fist emerging out of a factory chimney.

"The Fight Continues," it read.

Daniel Cohn-Bendit held up a bullhorn and shouted into it. "Your union, the CGT, says that we are risking a police reaction by coming here, but unlike your CGT we're not here to lead you, or to issue commands. The workers know well enough what they must do. We just bring our solidarity."

Gerrard wondered if he had ever left the police museum, or if he might wake up on the Metro. He'd find himself staring out at yellow tiles on the walls of Gare du Nord. The Flins workers were arriving in buses, and the students were handing out leaflets to them, one at a time. Most were glad to take what was offered. Most of the workers joined the demonstration.

The Renault factory workers in safety goggles and overalls locked arms with students and professors. They joined arms and blocked the street in an attempt to stop the buses bringing in scabs. Only the buses didn't carry scab workers, but soldiers. The men on the buses were armed with tear gas canisters, plastic shields, and batons. They disembarked and assembled. They were carrying what Gerrard thought were machine guns with crazy nozzles, but when they aimed the guns into the crowd and pulled the triggers he was relieved to find out that they were tear gas launchers.

The police marched on the crowd, pushed the workers up to the roundabout in the centre of Elizabethville, about half a kilometer from the Renault factory. A CGT official stood in the back of a pickup truck and exhorted the workers to abandon the picket and return to work. The CGT fully supported the rule of law and they were working to win the upcoming elections. Continued adventures, he said, undermined their chance for victory at the ballot box.

Tear gas spread across the crowd. The workers put on their goggles. Gerrard reached out blindly.

"Natalie?" he yelled.

She grabbed Gerrard around the waist with her right arm, and he turned around to see her react to the gas. She had one hand over her mouth and nose and was holding on to his belt with the other. Tears ran down her cheeks. Gerrard pointed to his palm, but she didn't understand the gesture, so he leaned in close to her and shouted.

"It's not real," Gerrard shouted. He started to take a flyer from his back pocket to show her that the words would change, that the centre would not hold, but then remembered he was dreaming and that she wasn't really there.

Gerrard stepped toward the police line, weaved through the plumes of gas. He stood next to a soldier in a black gas mask, kneeled so that he could see his reflection in the plastic shield the soldier was carrying. The image reflected there was not his own, but rather was the reflection of a young boy with a girl's haircut. The boy was wearing khaki knickers, a knitted jacket, and leather sandals.

As Gerrard bent down to look closer, to get a better look at the image of Christopher Robin, his legs sank into the ground.

Gerrard scooped up handfuls of clay, and stood up again. He smiled at Natalie and told her what was happening.

"This is a dream," he said.

Now he was six. Movement was impossible.

Gerrard opened his eyes.

29

On June 7, 1968, Natalie and Gerrard considered the propaganda posters on the gates outside the School of Fine Arts. Natalie chuckled over a poster where the artist had put Pompidou's head on the body of a chicken, and Gerrard stood stunned in front of an image of a helmeted policeman with a wrench in his mouth. The cartoon policeman resembled nothing so much as the skull and bones symbol for poison, and the words "Renault Flins" were written underneath his obscene face.

"What's happening at the Flins factory?" Gerrard asked.

Natalie started to answer, looked embarrassed, and then took a newspaper out of a paper bag she happened to be carrying.

A few workers in goggles came up from behind them and looked over Natalie's shoulder, as Natalie read the news aloud.

"The workers provoked the police, and while the department has released a statement of regret and condolences there will be no apology," the blonde read.

"What's that?" Gerrard asked. He grabbed the paper away

from Natalie, but what he saw wasn't a headline about the striking workers or de Gaulle.

"University students copulate in convertible," he read. Under the headline there was an essay describing the details.

"Wait." Natalie put her hands on her chest. She was wearing the same red gown from the night of the barricades, and she unbuttoned it and let it slip off her shoulders and fall to the ground. She exposed the propaganda poster she'd been hiding underneath her clothes.

The policeman on the poster was wearing a helmet and goggles so that his face looked like a skull. The wrench in his mouth might have been a bone.

According to Freud the contents of dreams are repressed desires from one's waking life, but Gerrard's waking life seemed very far away and what he really desired was to wake up.

Tear gas billowed out from the wrought-iron gate of the School of Fine Arts. The posters on the metal pillar burst into flames; cartoon fists and kepis and factories burned away. Police with plastic shields and batons came out of the fog and Gerrard turned and ran.

Blinking and falling, he found himself standing by a black pickup truck outside the Renault factory. Daniel Cohn-Bendit was standing in the bed of the truck, holding up a color poster of a smiling family by a pristine blue lake in one hand and a bullhorn in the other. Cohn-Bendit examined the bullhorn as if he weren't quite sure what it was, but he still looked quite sporty in his pink windbreaker and green dress shirt. He waved at Gerrard and then pointed toward an alley where Gerrard could see a few other students were already headed.

"That's the way back," Cohn-Bendit said. He held up the bullhorn and counted into it. *"Uno, dos, tres,"* he said. And they all ran to an open factory door on the west side of the building. Behind the concrete walls the factory was grey and old, like something left out in the rain and now half-rotten. It was already a ruin even though it was operational. The floors in the Renault factory were made from perfect flat clay. Gerrard took his first step and his foot was stuck. He took another step and realized that the walls were made of paper. The factory was phony.

Dreams weren't simply unconscious impulses presented as images. They worked themselves out through a metonymic chain of associations. What did the word factory stand in for? Production? Work? Power? Father?

Gerrard looked around for help. He called out for Natalie, for Christopher Robin, and then thought of calling for his dream mother, but realized that he didn't know her name.

Maybe he was in a swimming pool underwater, or maybe he'd fallen asleep in class at lycée?

Gerrard held up his left hand so he could look at his knuckles. But his hand was transparent. He could see the walls of the factory, the machine parts and gears that were spinning out life for him, on the other side.

Gerrard looked through his hand and then tried, again, to wake up. He opened his eyes.

29

Gerrard opened his eyes to pipes and wires, to the fluorescent bulbs and aluminum-framed windows of the interior of the Renault factory. He was lying on the floor inside the factory, and he stood up, brushed grit from the concrete floor off his tweed jacket, and looked to the left and then the right to get his bearings. He wanted an exit. Gerrard studied the yellow line that divided the hallway in half and decided to follow it. He could hear wheels turning and a repetitive electric beeping from overhead. Someone was driving a forklift and there were people working above him. Gerrard decided to seek them out. He wanted to find them before the police found him.

Gerrard was dreaming, but the dream was not his own. Gerrard had thought that knowing that it was a dream, that lucid thought, would be enough, but the dream had a structure, and there were dream police.

He didn't see them before they hit him. The first blow knocked him off his feet and onto his back. There were three policemen standing over him, each one seemingly seven feet tall, so big that they moved with clumsy deliberateness. They spoke to each other in mechanical clicks, and Gerrard couldn't see their faces under their goggles. When one swung his baton the others followed, each tracing the same arc in the air with the tip of his club, each hitting Gerrard with equal force.

First they struck him on the head, then on his ribs, and then, as he turned over and tried to crawl away, they cracked his spine. Gerrard stopped feeling the blows after that. He saw one of the police step on his right hand, crushing the bones, but he didn't feel it happen and he wasn't angry.

Gerrard forgot that he was dreaming. He tried to turn over to look at the police again, to let them know there were no hard feelings. He tried to bring his hand up to protect his face from the beating that continued, but he couldn't move. He lay on the concrete, and blood oozed out and colored his view of the yellow line so that it appeared orange. Another blow fell on his head, and another. Gerrard shut his eyes.

The dream wasn't his anymore. He had to wake up.

29

Gerrard opened his eyes and found himself on his stomach outside the Renault factory. Lying in a field, he could see blades of grass next to his head. He followed the green lines until he saw the sun, and then he looked down and waited for the moment to come into focus. He shifted his weight to see how bad the pain would be, to see if he could bend his back, and found he could do it. He sat up slowly and touched his head with both hands. There was no blood, or any other trace of what he'd imagined had happened.

He sat in the grass and considered it, listening for the other students, for the workers who were still on strike, but the sunlit world was quiet. There was nobody near him, just the tall grass, and off in the distance the dark windows of the factory's west side. He tried to remember how he'd gotten outside again, when he'd fallen asleep in the field, but quickly gave up when all that came to him were images from inside the factory. All that came to him were memories of the flat terrain of his dreams, the soft and malleable earth of dreamtime.

He stood up and found the view of the factory blocked by plumes of tear gas. He heard the sounds of footsteps on gravel. The sight of police on the road sent a wave of panic through him. He lay back down again, got onto his belly, and began to crawl. He set out for the factory.

Gerrard wanted to wake up. He wanted to remember himself, to bring something forward from the past to correct the present, but as he made his way forward into the grass he held his breath and found that he did not really need to breathe.

The police saw him. Maybe a dozen men in helmets, and brandishing nightsticks, were pushing their way through the field of wheat toward him. They were cutting a straight line forward. Each step followed the last in an irreversible chain of cause and effect.

Gerrard stood up and started running, and the men behind him let out yells, commanding him to stop. They shot more tear gas grenades at him, but it was a simple thing to hold his breath as he reached the factory gates.

"The boy is there," the policeman yelled. Gerrard turned to look at where they were coming from, to gauge the distance between them, and saw that they were still a long way off. They were pushing through the grass, but not getting any closer. He turned back to the gate, but did not rush. A gas canister exploded ahead of him, and he held his breath. It was painful to keep his eyes open, but he had to do it. He tried to open his eyes wider and wider.

29

Gerrard opened his mouth and tasted mud and then opened his eyes. The police were still after him. He'd fallen, slipped in the mud by the river.

He stood and started running, and then slipped again, tumbled back down into it, and they were on him.

The police beat him with their clubs. They hit him methodically, as if they were hammering a nail.

Gerrard had to wake up. They were going to kill him otherwise. Gerrard stood up, and the police pushed him forward, into the water.

In the grey of the Seine Gerrard opened his eyes, and for just a moment he saw the outline of a window. He opened his eyes and saw sunlight coming into a dusty room.

He was in a poster bed in a hotel room on Rue du Four and Natalie was lying there next to him. They were both on top of the sheets and Natalie was naked and shivering.

Gerrard asked her what time it was, but before she could answer he had to breathe. He opened his mouth to let in air and tasted river water.

29

Gerrard opened his eyes and found he was underwater. He was being held underwater. He saw the faces of the police rippling above him. They were using their clubs and hands to hold him down, and he struggled. He kicked and bit and thrashed.

And then, before he could wake up again, before he could open his eyes again, water rushed into his mouth. He felt the struggle pass out of him as the cold water seeped in.

Gerrard drowned.

30

On June 13 all the student groups that had formed during the strike were declared illegal and hundreds of students and young workers were arrested en masse. Natalie, however, was not among them. Instead she spent the day at Café Charbon reading and rereading the front page of *L'Humanité*. She felt sick. No matter how many times she tried the trick the words remained the same.

Two days earlier she'd attended her last demonstration, this one in protest called by Les Détournés with the words "A Comrade Is Dead." After Gerrard had drowned, after the demonstration at the Flins factory had gone wrong, Les Détournés had made him over as a martyr.

"Comrade Hand: from now on your name is inseparable from the popular revolution, from our people's springtime!" Their flyer had called for unity, for taking up and continuing the struggle, but Natalie couldn't continue that way. She didn't know what she would do next, or even what she wanted to do. She sat at Café Charbon for hours, first drinking coffee and then gin. She was wearing one of Abby Milne's tweed wool skirts and an oversized chiffon blouse that made her feel small. She'd thought she might go back to Nanterre where her own clothes were, or head back to her parents' apartment in Suresnes, but she had no idea where she'd go from there. She doubted that her day dresses and American blue jeans would fit her any better than Abby Milne's clothes did. She had the idea that nothing would quite fit her again.

Guy Debord and Isadora Baris were at the table next to hers playing a game they'd invented using flags and castles and a hundred little squares on a wooden board. They seemed grotesque to Natalie, like spoiled children. They strategized and played with their toys when they ought to be weeping or at least getting drunk.

"I'm not the only one who has lost someone," Natalie said to Guy. She leaned in close to him and whispered in his ear while she stared at Isadora. She rubbed her cheek against his and then said it again. "There are hundreds of us. Hundreds whose lovers died with the occupation."

Isadora watched Natalie, met her eye, but didn't say anything. Isadora moved her flag, and Guy retaliated. They both continued playing their game.

A few drinks later, once she was sure she was drunk, Natalie stepped out onto the street, which was wet from the drizzling rain. Paris smelled good to her. She stood on a narrow curb along Rue Descartes and leaned against a round red sign with a white dash. The sign read NO ENTRY.

Natalie continued on despite this. She walked along the concrete embankment of the Seine on the right bank, only occasionally stopping to look into the grey water, only occasionally allowing herself to think of what it would be like to be stuck down there, to drown there, in the muck.

The insurrections, dreams, and love affairs of the summer were over and it was still June. She was nineteen and it was clear that her chance to live had passed. There was nothing left to reverse, no next step to take.

On the other side of the Pont Marie a city worker was scrubbing the walls underneath the bridge in an effort to erase the graffiti and the memory of May, but there was still enough of a visible remainder for Natalie to read out the message.

"'Rather life,'" she read. She repeated it over and over again softly by the Seine, and she waited for something to rise in her that she could call to by name. "Rather life," she said.

31

At home Christopher felt like a tourist. Rather than take his spot behind the cash register he wandered between the bookshelves and looked at the titles on the spines. He noticed how the books in the gardening section all had green covers, while history books were brown. His bookshop was color coded. Christopher pulled books off the shelves: J. D. Salinger, Jackie Collins, and A. A. Milne. He reshelved these in the gardening section in order to put a vertical splotch of red and brown in the center of the row of green spines.

He took his cardboard box of anomalies out from his bedroom closet and looked them over. He wasn't sure if he wanted to dispose of the orange poster and toy cat, or if he wanted to put the toy donkey he'd brought back with him, the green poster that depicted a herd of sheep and the slogan "Retour a la Normale" into the box with the rest of the oddities.

Later, they had lunch at home. Daniel refused to eat and instead arranged his cheese and crackers in a straight line on his plate. Christopher ate apple slices and toast with jam, something he'd quickly prepared for himself. He made himself a cup of tea with cream, and Abby served herself reheated oatmeal with milk and honey. There was no conversation but just eating, stacking, and thinking. Christopher thought the space in the little kitchen seemed false, and that they were all of them just barely going through the motions of what had been everyday life before. The linoleum kitchen table, the wooden blinds, and even the sunlight streaming in, all of it seemed a bit contrived.

"Let's get away from the store for today," Christopher suggested. "It's no good acting like nothing has happened."

They took the ferry from the quay to Dartmouth Castle. Christopher was pleased by the smell of the Dart and the way the wind whipped across the surface of the river. He was pleased when the other tourists had to grab their sunhats and close their eyes. The women across from him were color coded just like his books. One was wearing a red knit skirt, the next wore yellow slacks, and the girl with them wore an argyle sweater and blue jeans. The lot of them ducked down below the edge of the boat, while Christopher and his family sat like statues with their eyes open. The red, yellow, and light blue houses made from Dutch brick, as well as the green hills and trees behind these, seemed to be moving away from them, but it was the ferry boat that was really drifting away from the quay.

Abby spoke into the wind and Christopher had to lean toward her and cup his left ear in order to hear.

". . . misunderstood the slogan," she said.

"What slogan?"

" 'Underneath the cobblestones, the beach.' "

When the students had pried cobblestones free from the streets they'd found sand underneath, but what their slogan implied was that freedom could be found immediately. All that was required in order for the students to liberate themselves was this spontaneous collective effort in the street. They just had to remove the cobblestones.

"For most of them it was all too hormonal. They wanted the beach. They wanted a seaside vacation and Brigitte Bardot in a bikini. They wanted to make a revolution based only on freedom and pleasure," Abby said. "But there was something else. There is another way to interpret the word 'beach.' "

"Yes."

"Christopher, a beach is what one storms. What's underneath the cobblestones is not Bardot's beach, but a beachhead."

When they reached the castle Daniel and Abby had to use the toilet. Chris waited outside the souvenir shop, passing the time by looking over the activity book that had come with their tickets.

Saint Petrox Church was built in 1170, two centuries before the fortress was built at Mayor Hawley's suggestion, and then Saint Petrox was incorporated into the fortress. A hundred years later the French threat compelled the addition of a gun tower. The fortress was built for cannons and the activity book suggested that one keep an eye out for "murder holes."

Christopher looked up at the tower and was impressed by it. The structure had lasted even if the world it was built to protect had not. The time for kings and queens had passed, but the high stone walls and crenellations were standing. The people who'd built Dartmouth Castle had been confident of their right to defend their way of life.

When Daniel and Abby emerged from the lavatories Chris

suggested they head for the main structure, which included both Saint Petrox Church and the gun tower.

Inside the church the gold inlay in the high ceiling reflected light so that even the pale marble columns showed an orange tinge.

Daniel remembered to whisper as he looked up at the large stained-glass window behind the altar. The glass kept the church safe and separate from the cold sky outside.

"What about the umbrella?" Daniel echoed television. "What about the Woodentops?"

When they passed the first set of strong doors Daniel let out a gasp and ran to the far left corner of the vast chamber. He ran along and reached out so that he could feel the texture of the rough walls. His left palm was filthy by the time he reached the cannon.

"This makes a loud noise," he said.

They spent their first day back in just this way.

Christopher might return to his bookstore, and he could return to his old habits, but he would have to choose to return. And he'd have to keep on choosing. He'd have to choose every day. Somehow Christopher had ended up on the surface of his daily life.

When they returned to the Harbour Bookshop later that night Chris found a red-and-white soda can along the boardwalk and stopped to pick it up. He held the diamond-patterned Coke can and considered what he wanted to do with it while his wife and son waited for him to unlock the door.

"Wait a moment," Christopher said.

"What is it?"

"I'd like to try something," Christopher said.

"What?" Abby asked.

"I would like to play a game of Pooh Sticks."

Christopher collected garbage and debris as substitutes. He gave Abby a red straw and Daniel received a green-and-white wax paper cup. Then the three of them walked back to the quay and out on the floating cedar dock for the sailboats. They stopped in a spot between the plastic floats attached underneath the cedar planks of the dock, and they all three got on hands and knees in order to set their objects into the water in the exact spot necessary so that the current might sweep the junk all the way to the other side.

Christopher, Abby, and Daniel said "Ready steady go!" in unison, and dropped the cola can, the straw, and the paper cup into the River Dart. They watched the garbage get sucked underneath the dock, and then crossed to the other side and waited.

Daniel started humming tunelessly. "Ready-steady-go!" he repeated. "Ready-steady-go!"

The five sailboats along the floating dock across from them all had white sails, but the boats themselves were color coded just like the books in his shop, just like the tourists on the ferry.

Christopher watched the spot where the Pooh Sticks should emerge and wondered who would win, but as the minutes passed it became obvious that none of the debris was going to reappear.

"Well that didn't work," Christopher said. "And we can't just leave that garbage under the dock."

"No?" Abby asked.

Christopher lay down on the cedar planks, edged out over the river, and then reached for the gap. Abby sat on his legs while Christopher bent at the waist and put his hand down and felt where river algae had built up on the plastic floats. He reached into the gap and hoped that something, maybe the straw, would somehow be stuck just under the dark water, but rather than feeling plastic or tin Christopher fingered what felt like hair.

Christopher grabbed hold of what turned out to be the yellow fur of his stuffed bear. He pulled it out of the water and shouted out to Abby to grab his belt and pull. Then Christopher straightened out and, when he was facedown on the dock, he rolled over and sat up.

"Look what was under there," Christopher said.

"A silly old bear," Abby said.

"Silly old bear," Daniel echoed.

Christopher held up the toy, looked the pudgy bear over, and then handed him to Daniel. "Careful," he said. "He's water logged and fragile. Be careful."

Daniel held Christopher's stuffed toy and smiled. And there, on the docks of the River Dart, after a Coke can had been lost and replaced by his old stuffed bear, and after everyday life in Devon had proven to be elusive, Christopher Robin watched his son play with this wet Pooh, and wondered when the students of Paris, the shopkeepers of Dartsmouth, or the children of their children might decide to look for the North Pole again.

Douglas Lain has had a number of short stories published. His podcast, *Diet Soap,* has been entertaining visitors for several years. *Billy Moon* is his first novel. He lives with his family in Portland, Oregon.

Discover more at <u>www.douglaslain.com</u>.